CRIME & CREEPS

A Short Story Collection

A V IAIN

Contents

DRAGON ON THE HILL

1

MILDRED STOOD OUT behind her hillside cabin, washing her hands in chilly water which pumped through a groaning and creaking tap. Gravel crunched up the path. Mildred wiped her hands on the sides of her apron and stepped in through the back door. She brought the folding counter down, making the hinges creak, and waited.

Two teenagers, a boy and a girl, stepped into the cabin. No greetings, just a pair of grunts. They wore hats with earmuffs and bomber jackets, hands stuffed into the pockets. The boy had a pierced nose and the strap of the girl's white undershirt was visible above the neckline of her jacket. A mixture of deodorant and perfume prickled Mildred's nostrils.

City people.

Mildred looked between the two of them. "May I help you?"

The girl snorted. "Got gum?"

"No."

The girl shrugged, glanced at the boy.

Mildred reached under the counter and felt the smooth wooden rifle stock. She ran her fingertips over the name engraved there. It felt warm, secure. She unclasped the buckles holding the rifle in place. "You'd better be going then. It's getting late. You won't be able to get up the ridge and back before night."

The boy chewed his lower lip, eyed Mildred and then reached inside his jacket, producing a handgun. He held his arm straight and pointed it at Mildred's chest. "Listen, bitch, we know about the gold, so hand it the fuck over."

Mildred wrapped her fingers around the rifle, still below the counter, and eyed the boy. "What gold?"

The boy flinched, wiped a strand of snot from his nose with

3

his free hand and stepped closer. The gun shook in his grasp. "Don't act stupid, you old cunt. We know all about it."

The girl took a step back. "Danny? This is too much. Let's go, Danny."

The boy shook his head. "Nah, we're finishing this. Didn't come out all this way for nuffink."

Mildred felt the weight of the rifle in her grip and her eyes wandered upward, above the two children, to the portrait of her husband. It hung a little crooked. She would have to rehang it later.

"Oy! Are you senile or what? Get a fucking move on!"

Mildred brought her focus back to the boy. He had a steely gaze but his watering eyes gave him away. He had never killed before. She was sure of it. A child who overstepped the mark needed to be punished.

She ducked down, slipped the rifle off its hooks, cocked it. The boy fired. His bullet whizzed past her ear and bit into the cabin wall. Wood chips caught in her hair. She rose, straightened her arm, looked along the sight and shot the boy right between the eyes. He toppled backward and crumpled to the floor.

Mildred reloaded. The girl's lips parted to scream. Mildred shot her too, the body falling beside the boy's. Mildred stared at the pair of them. Each had a gaping hole in the head. A pair of bloody pools formed beneath their skulls.

Keeping the rifle crooked beneath her arm, she flipped the counter up onto its hinges and examined the bodies. She gave each a nudge with her foot. Satisfied they were dead, she sighed, placed the rifle on the counter and then closed the cabin shutters.

2

S HE DUG A GRAVE in the forest out back. When night fell she dragged the bodies, one at a time, through long grass to the hole. With them nestled inside, she rested on the shovel a moment to catch her breath and then packed dirt on top, covering the disturbed earth with dead leaves.

Back in the cabin, she took care of the bloodstains on the wooden boards—they scrubbed nicely into the wood grain—and then she tucked herself into bed, switching to the classical music station on the radio. That night she slept soundly, dreaming of her husband.

3

A HARSH RAPPING at the cabin door brought Mildred round. She shucked off the covers and opened up. Mr Finley stood at the threshold, a smile on his lips, wrinkles marking his forehead. He ran a bed and breakfast in the nearby village of Sesney. "Good morning, Mrs Cartwright."

"Good morning."

He wrinkled his nose and scratched the back of his neck. "I had some guests come up here yesterday and they never returned last night. You didn't see a boy and girl, did you?"

She pouted. "I'm afraid not."

"Ah."

"You see I've been unwell the past day or so, in bed."

Finley nodded along. "Yes, I thought it strange you hadn't opened this morning. You . . ." he paused as if he regretted starting the sentence and then continued, "You are okay up here, all alone, aren't you? It's just that I had a funny feeling about those children. Well"—he drew closer and spoke more quietly —"I looked amongst their belongings and turned up what I believe to be drugs. I informed the police at once, of course."

Mildred sighed, shaking her head. "It's terrible the type who have found us out here, isn't it?"

"Quite."

"Anyway, you've no need to worry about me, Mr Finley. Jeremy takes care of me."

"Jeremy?"

"My husband."

"Oh, right, that's . . . then . . . yes." Mr Finley scratched the back of his neck again, looked off down the trail. "Terribly sorry to bother you. I'd better get back into town, inform mountain rescue." He stepped back, tripped over a rock but caught himself on the portico. "Silly me!" He set foot back on the path. "You will let me know if you see those kids, won't you?"

"I haven't a phone, Mr Finley, and I wouldn't like to walk into town, all that way and back again, with my brittle bones, just to tell you that I've seen some snotty-nosed children who are most likely on their way back down."

He widened his eyes, cleared his throat and then forced a smile. "Yes, perfectly right, Mrs Cartwright. Please don't exert yourself on their behalf. Not worth it. Still, they are guests and I must do the right thing."

"It seems so."

"Goodbye, Mrs Cartwright," he said, and then set off at a frantic pace back toward Sesney.

THE NEXT DAY mountain rescue teams scoured the area up the ridge, an hour's walk from Mildred's cabin. Mildred served them refreshments on the way up, watching various pieces of equipment passing up and down the trail. In the afternoon they brought in a helicopter, which chopped over the trail for hours, and a dog squad which also failed to pick up a scent. A week later mountain rescue abandoned their search.

So much fuss for a pair of scroungers.

Mildred returned to her routine: serving refreshments to families with dogs, middle-aged couples, the right sort. As she handed over a chocolate bar to a walker, she noticed a pair of uniformed men approaching her cabin. Police officers. She had lived up in the cabin for over thirty years and in that time she had never seen a police officer, almost forgotten they existed.

One of the police officers continued up the slope while the other made for her cabin. He had a buzz-cut and his sweat-soaked shirt collar dug into his neck. "Mrs Cartwright, I presume?"

"That's right."

He held out his hand. "Officer Mills."

"Pleased to meet you. I suppose you're here about the missing children?"

"Exactly, madam." He withdrew a notepad, slapped it on the counter and then glanced around the cabin. When he noticed her husband's picture he squinted. "That man looks familiar." He glanced back at Mildred. "Is he a singer or something?"

Mildred flushed a little. "My husband."

He turned to face her, eyes lingering on hers. "Is he—?"

She pursed her lips, nodded.

"I'm sorry. I didn't realise."

"Why else should I be out here all alone?"

"Yes, it makes sense now."

She paced over to the hot water pot. "Tea, officer?"

He accepted it with thanks, withdrew a pen from his shirt pocket and then flipped to a clean page in his notepad. "This shouldn't take long. What I understand from talking to people in town is that you didn't see the kids. Is that correct?"

"Yes, officer."

He scribbled a note.

"Where have you come from this morning, officer?"

"The city," he said.

"And you plan to go back today?"

"Yes, I think so. Don't plan on staying in Sesney overnight if we can help it." He sipped his tea, wincing a little at the temperature. "It doesn't look like we're going to turn up much here. What chance do a couple of officers have if a mountain rescue team found no trace?"

"Quite right."

"Still, got to put together a report. Cross the t's, dot the i's, you know how it is. Between you and me, after talking to the kids' families back in the city, they sound like nothing more than a pair of punks. Last kind you'd expect to find out here, in the country-side. Probably don't even know the difference between a cow and a sheep."

Mildred chuckled.

He pulled back his sleeve and scrutinised his watch. "All going well we'll be back in the city by the early-evening. Got a table booked. It's my wife's birthday. You can't imagine the fuss she kicked up when I told her that I had to come way out here." He feigned biting his knuckles. "Fire and brimstone, let me tell you."

"Oh dear."

Mills knocked back his tea and set the cup on the counter. "Thank you very much, Mrs Cartwright." He headed for the door and then stopped halfway, patted down his pockets. He turned back, noticed his notepad on the counter, smiled, picked it up and slipped it into his pocket. "Would've got into quite a bit of trouble if I'd left that here."

Mildred smiled.

He hovered. "There was one thing I wanted to ask."

"Go ahead."

"A silly thing, really, but I suppose I should while I'm here."

"Please, officer, I'm much too old to be embarrassed."

"This morning I was speaking to Mr Finley, where the children were staying, and he mentioned overhearing them speaking about gold that they believed you kept up here in the cabin."

A hot rush passed through Mildred. She forced herself to remain calm. "Is that so?"

"And, well, although it hadn't occurred to Mr Finley at the time, it seems likely that they might've set out on the trail to come and rob you."

She clutched her hand to her throat. "Rob me?"

"Yes." He sighed. "But that can't be the case. I mean, the trail leading up here is straightforward enough. I couldn't imagine getting lost, and I've got the sense of direction of a lemming. No, they must be up over the ridge."

"Sounds likely to me."

Mills headed back for the door, taking in the picture again, and then shaking his head. "That face is so familiar to me. I'm sure I've seen it before."

"A lot of people say that."

"Perhaps it's just the style, you know"—he waved his hand over his face—"like the moustache and hair."

"That must be it."

"Thank you, Mrs Cartwright. And sorry for intruding."

"That's perfectly all right, officer. I hope you make it back to the city in time for your reservations."

"Yes, I hope so too." He smiled and then headed out of the door, up the trail, after his partner.

Mildred stood at the counter, staring into thin air and turning over the recent events in her mind. And then she glanced up at her husband, beaming back at her, and she felt a weight lift off her shoulders.

5

THAT NIGHT, outside the cabin, there was a sound of scuffling. Mildred glanced up from her book, a hardbound Victorian romance which had earlier formed part of a much larger collection. She set the book down on the counter, marking her page, and got to her feet, snatching up the rifle as she went.

She stepped into a pair of wellies and then opened the back door. She peered around the area, unable to make out anything other than shapes in the gloom. And then a figure a matter of a few steps from where she stood, shifted through the darkness. Heart drumming in her ears, she cocked the rifle and brought the sight up to her eye. "Who's there?"

The crunch of footsteps across crispy ground ceased. "Officer Mills."

She gritted her teeth and kept the rifle raised. "You're trespassing. This is private property."

His form twisted through the gloom, drawing closer. A light blinked on at his side and he shone the torch, temporarily blinding her. "Lower the gun, Mrs Cartwright."

She hesitated and then did as he said.

Mills drew closer still and withdrew something from his pocket. He got up close, a few steps away. "May we talk inside?"

Mildred nodded and then stood aside, to allow him past.

6

MILLS DREW UP a wooden chair and sat. He wore a fleecy jumper and a pair of sturdy boots. Not on duty. He brushed away at the object in his hand. Mildred recognised it as a hat which had belonged to one of the children. It must've dropped off one of the bodies as she carried it to the grave.

Mills eyed her. "I found this, out in the woods." His focus shifted to the rifle. "Please, lay the gun down."

Mildred clutched the gun tighter.

"Mrs Cartwright, I radioed my partner. He's on his way up the trail. It's all over."

She raised the gun, pointed it between his eyes, just like she had with the children. Another body, another person gone. It made no difference if it kept her secret safe.

Mills remained unmoved. "It's not the first time I've had a loaded gun pointed at me, you know." He placed the hat on the counter, glanced up at her husband's picture and then tugged at the loose skin around his fingernails. "I remembered where I saw that picture. In the files, back at the academy, an unsolved mystery."

Her finger tightened against the trigger.

"Quite a suspicious end. Up and disappeared."

"And?"

He stared into her eyes. "You came off quite well following his disappearance, didn't you? Took all his property and assets. No other family. Children from his first marriage disinherited."

"And what about it?"

A smile tweaked the corner of his mouth. "May I ask why you live here, at the backend of beyond? Why you no longer use your title, Lady Cartwright?"

"Because I want to be far away from everyone. From all of that."

He yawned, stretched his arms. "You know, it's been a long day. Been all the way to the city and back. A real shame considering that the mansion is just crumbling away."

"I wouldn't know. I haven't left this cabin for thirty years."

"Well, a few years ago the estate passed into the hands of the council. They believed all Lord Cartwright's family to be dead so they built houses on the land. The kids that came here live in one of those houses."

Cracks appeared in her resolve. All the memories coming back. Her moment of madness. Now it seemed so petty.

He chuckled. "I had a good root through the kids' things. They found receipts in the mansion: for this cabin, for the gold. You left in a hurry, didn't you, Lady Cartwright?"

It felt as if the lettering on the rifle stock burned her skin. Her hands shook and then she lowered the rifle, let it rest on the counter. "Don't address me by that name."

Mills picked up the hat and turned it over in his hands, as if examining the needlework. "What puzzles me more is why you killed those kids and buried them out in the woods. You don't seem to have any need for the gold, in this condition."

A chill settled over her chest.

He stood. "I found the grave. Tomorrow we'll exhume them and I'm certain we will find that the bullets in their bodies match that rifle right there. You're going to prison for what you did, so why not admit what you did to your husband, have some peace?" His eyes froze onto hers and then he approached the rifle, rested his hand on it. "May I?"

Tears pooled in the corners of her eyes. She nodded.

Mills picked up the rifle, popped the bullet free. It clinked onto the floor. He checked it over. "Quite an old thing, this. Never seen one so old myself, not in working order." He noticed the stock and held it up to the electric lamp to read the name, inscribed in gold. "Jeremy H Cartwright. This was your husband's?"

"Yes."

"But yours now?"

Not a day had passed by when she had not regretted what she'd done. "Yes."

"Why did you kill him?"

Mills was right. She had to give herself some peace, admit her mistakes. A knot formed in her throat. She swallowed it back. "I loved him so much. But . . . but you should have seen how he let good potential go to waste. He bought idiot things: cars, boats, an aeroplane, expensive suits, stupid holidays abroad. I wanted to restore the estate, bring it back to its former beauty. And . . . and then, he told me he wanted to sell it. So . . . so I—" She sobbed. "I took the money and ran. No one could know me."

"Where's his body?"

She stayed very still and then crossed the room, crouched down, and peeled back several floorboards. Mills laid the rifle back down and stood over her. She peeled back more and more until almost the entire floor was bare. Gold bars glittered in the light.

Lying between them was a body, wrapped in white cloth, like a pharaoh en route to the afterlife.

LODGER

1

VERY FEW THINGS sent a tremble down Violet's spine.
But a knocking on the door—in the dead of night—
was one of those.

Violet turned over on her too-thin mattress, listening to the
slink and *strain* of the coiled-up springs of her camp bed. The
camp bed which was supposed to last her all the way through till
spring. She could smell the rust off it . . . could *taste* the rust of it
in her mouth.

She peered out into the darkness surrounding her—her mind
still ebbing back, away from sleep, and towards the real world.

She reached downwards for the torch she always kept beside
her bed, and she flicked it on with a practised motion.

There was another round of knocks at the door.

This time harder—*louder*.

To try and stop her legs from shaking out from underneath
her, Violet mumbled to herself, "I'm coming, I'm coming," as if
that might put the person knocking at her door to rest.

She walked barefoot over the bare, wooden planks of the
lodge—nothing more than a kitchen, living area and a bedroom.
A single storey. Out here, in the middle of the woods. She wore a
thick fleece on top, and a pair of waterproof trousers underneath
as she always did to sleep. Under all *those* layers, of course, she
also had her pyjamas, and, on those especially cold nights—
nights like tonight—she even wore thermal underneath beneath
it all too.

When she reached the door, she held still, the torch dangling
from her hand, shining its yellow circle at her feet, and she sniffed
a little. "Who is it?" she said.

There was no reply.

She realised that she had spoken quietly.

In almost a whisper.

There was no wonder the person on the other side of the door hadn't heard her.

She cleared her throat and then spoke louder. "Who is it?" she said.

This time, on the other side of the door, she heard a stirring. "Gotta guy injured here, can we bring him in?"

Violet reached out and felt for the doorknob, but she held back before turning it—telling herself that she had to be a little more cautious here, had to pay attention to her gut instinct. "Injured how?" she said.

"He got shot, miss."

Violet felt her heart thump loudly in her ears, her hands seem to grow impossibly cold. Something about this—*all of this*—just didn't seem right. She glanced about herself as if the darkness which pressed up against her on all sides would offer an excuse.

"I . . . I don't have much here," she said. "Not much in the way of medical supplies."

There was a grumble on the other side of the door, and then the reply came, "Miss, that doesn't matter, we need to get this guy here to shelter, okay?"

Violet held off for another couple of moments, and then, realising that—if they really wanted—they could bust the door right down, she let them in.

THERE WERE THREE MEN. All of them wore hunting jackets. The one in the middle, Violet saw right away from the way the other two supported him, was injured. She could smell the dank odour of blood straightaway.

She stepped back, away from them, and they piled on in past her.

The electric light out on the porch which shone all night, illuminated enough of the living area of the lodge—enough so that the men could lay their companion down on the rug.

One of the uninjured men, and the same one who had spoken to her from outside the door, Violet could tell from the resonance of his voice, asked if she could switch on some more lights, so that they'd have a better chance of seeing what they had here.

Violet did as they asked, going out back to flip on the generator. She switched it off at night both to save fuel and because she couldn't standing the constant buzzing—that buzzing made it impossible to sleep. That was why she kept the torch beside her bed so that she would have something to cling to in the darkness.

When she returned to the lodge, peered in through the door and to the living area, she saw the main light had come on, and that the two men were stripping off their companion's hunting jacket.

Violet still felt like she was half clinging to dreamland. She felt numb all over, as if this scene before her might disappear in a moment, and she'd wake in the old, familiar darkness.

Have the urge to go to the toilet.

But she didn't wake up.

Thinking quickly, Violet shipped off into the kitchen, got hold of the first aid kit there and brought it to the two men. One of them cracked it open, pawed through it, and worked quickly, separating sutures, and hypodermic needles, and medical gauze . . . most of it stuff that Violet only really had a working knowledge of.

She was careful out here, in the woods, and since she was the only one at this station at this time in the season, she hadn't really had need to make use of much more than the occasional plaster, or a dab of antiseptic cream here or there.

A gunshot wound, though . . . that was a different matter altogether.

Something which, she was sure, was beyond the scope of the simple first aid kit.

Violet couldn't really think of how she could make herself useful, so she was glad when one of the men asked her to go off to the kitchen and boil up some water. She set the water to boil on the gas stove in the kitchen, and then returned to the living area.

She took in the men, and their hunting jackets, saw that they were all streaked in mud. She studied the two men helping their companion: one of them had blond hair poking out from beneath his beanie cap, while the other, who had shucked his beanie cap as he'd staggered into the lodge, had long, black hair which curled as it brushed his shoulders.

The injured man, lying flat on his back on the scrappy little rug of the living area, had a clean-shaven scalp. No sign of stubble whatsoever. Violet wondered if he shaved his head every morning, out here, in the woods.

When the water boiled, she mixed a little cold water into the saucepan, and then brought it through to the pair of men. They accepted it with rugged, embattled smiles, and Violet took up her spot on the periphery once more.

The men had perhaps been inside the lodge for half an hour before Violet's mind snapped back to protocol—to how she was supposed to treat situations like this. She had to call it in . . . call it in with the central lodge, about five kilometres away.

And so she headed into the kitchen, unhooked the walkie-talkie from its stand, and then switched it on. She set it calling and then stood in the doorway to the living area, watching on as the men worked to help their buddy out. Without really thinking, she said, "I'll try to get in touch with another of the lodges—they might be able to send out a search party. Doubt they'll be able to bring a chopper by, not really any place to set it down."

Neither of the men looked up at her, though the grunt she heard from the blond-haired one seemed to be a sign of approval.

Violet looked down on the injured man, saw how the other two had worked quickly on him, cut him free from his clothing so that he was now bare-chested as he lay on the rug. She saw the bullet hole, where he'd been shot, just above his left hip. It just oozed blood: black and thick, with a reddish tinge.

She felt her stomach crunch in on itself. She had never been the biggest fan of blood. She could remember a handful of incidents, back when she'd been taking her wilderness training, when she'd had to treat the odd cut or scrape, and even that had made her feel greatly uneasy.

Her attention returned to her walkie-talkie.

No answer yet.

She guessed that was par for the course, what with it being the middle of the night. She was sure that the warden would be fast asleep still, all tucked up in bed. She could never remember, herself, to leave her walkie-talkie beside her bed. She almost always seemed to leave it propped up on its charging stand, in the kitchen.

As she watched the men continue to work on their injured companion, her mind swam along, still in that dreamy state. She found herself speculating about the men, *wondering* to herself. And the thought she found herself wondering was just where the men's guns were, assuming that one of them had been the one to shoot . . . that was *always* what happened out here—whenever anybody took a gun along with them on a hunting party they *always* ended up shooting themselves.

Seeing that the men were occupied with the gunshot wound, Violet headed out the door of the lodge and glance about the façade, seeing if they'd maybe propped their guns up against the side. But, nope, there was no sign of a gun anywhere.

Feeling a little weirded-out by the whole thing, but mostly putting it down to still being a touch sleepy, she returned to the lodge, where the men working on their companion were now working at sticking down the gauze over the gunshot wound.

The blond man, kneeling up, sat back, and then glanced around at Violet.

His expression was grim, and his eyes appeared sunken in their sockets.

"You think we could wash up a little?" he said.

When Violet looked to the blond man, and then the man with the black hair, she saw that they both had blood all over their hands, and up to their wrists.

"Of course," she said, surprised that they had even bothered to ask, and then she pointed them off in the direction of the toilet.

They left their companion behind.

Left him with Violet.

She looked down at their injured companion, saw that his eyes had fluttered shut, but that his eyelids continued to flicker in a way that told her he was in pain—perhaps passing in and out of shock. She noticed that his cheeks had a slight blue tinge to them. She wanted to be able to do something for him, but she knew, what with them being out here, out in the wilderness, and coupled with her lack of medical know-how, there was really nothing to be done.

Nothing except getting him to a hospital ASAP.

Right as she heard the gush of taps from the sink in the toilet, at the other side of the lodge, the injured man's eyes flickered open. His eyes seemed to drink in the room surrounding him before they drifted over onto Violet's.

His expression became one of alarm, and his dry lips muttered something which Violet couldn't hear from where she stood in the doorway to the kitchen.

So she stooped down, approached him, listened hard to his rasping, stretched voice.

"When they go . . . when they *leave* . . . run . . . run *away!*"

3

VIOLET WAS STILL STOOPING OVER the injured man when the other two returned from their toilet trips. They'd spent quite a while getting their hands clean, but they seemed to have succeeded for the most part. She knew that it was a task to get anything clean with cold water, and that there wouldn't be any warm water till the tank had had a chance to heat up.

When she heard the blond man's voice over her shoulder, her heart leaped up to her throat, and she had half a thought that it might pop up into her mouth.

"He still out for the count?" the blond man said.

Violet spun around, looked into his eyes, saw the faint expression of curiosity there. She looked back at the injured man, still lying flat on the floor before her, saw that his eyes were once more shut, and then she replied, "Yeah, he's still asleep."

"Hmm," the blond man replied.

Violet took a couple of steps back, hoping to make it to the kitchen. She still hadn't received any response on her walkie-talkie, and she was keen, once the response came, to be out of earshot of these men. They were suspicious to say the least.

She had to slide past the blond man because he stood in the way—in the doorway to the kitchen. The other man, with the black hair, was just inside the kitchen. She guessed that it wasn't going to be as easy as she had thought to get herself alone with her walkie-talkie.

When Violet reached the stove, she looked back to the men and asked, "Can I make you something to eat at all?"

Neither of the men responded. Both of them remained fixed on the injured man still lying on the living space floorboards.

Deciding to go for a different approach, she said, "What were you doing out there—out in the forests?"

Another long pause and then the blond man shucked his silence in such a dramatic manner that it put Violet in mind of a machine gun with the trigger held down—spraying bullets all over the place. "We were out there, in the woods, because we were hunting. We have no licences. We parked up our van a little way off over that way"—he gestured in the direction, though Violet hardly had a chance to register it properly—"we've been knocking about here, camping, for a good few days. Not really got anybody monitoring this area, have you?"

Violet realised, from the fact that the man had stopped speaking, that she was supposed to put her oar in here. And so she did. "Uh, *I'm* monitoring this stretch."

"Yeah, well," the blond man continued, "Guess you're not doing much of a great job if reprobates like us can manage to sneak our way in to try and bag us some game, huh?"

Violet held very still, not quite sure what to say about all this. And then she decided that she should try to stick up for herself. "It's a big area," Violet said. "And we're understaffed. It's not like we can go sticking a whole bunch of people in every nook and cranny of the woodlands, is it?"

The blond man seemed to acknowledge this. She watched on as he reached into the pocket of his hunting jacket which he still wore, but unzipped now. He withdrew a pipe from the pocket and jabbed it between his lips.

"You can't *smoke* here," Violet said, surprising herself at her brutal tone.

"Go outside, shall I?" the blond man said.

Violet shook her head. "*No*, I mean that you can't smoke *anywhere* within the preserve—it's forbidden. You could start a forest fire."

The blond man exchanged glances with the black-haired

man. The blond man gave a shrug and then turned his attention back to Violet. "Huh, wish I'd known that a couple of days ago, when we got here."

Violet wasn't sure if the men were a little in shock at what had happened to their friend, or if they were intentionally being arseholes. Whichever it was, she was really starting to get pissed off. "So," she said, taking great effort to keep her tone cool, "You manage to bag anything at all on this hunting trip?"

This elicited another silence, and it wasn't long into it before Violet craved the sound of their voices again. It was funny, out here, in the middle of nowhere, human voices, whether they come along in the form of a crackling walkie-talkie, or as a sarky poacher, were somehow soothing to her.

The blond man was tapping tobacco into his pipe, apparently undeterred by Violet's warning. But, then again, what exactly was she going to do if he *did* break the rules? Would she place a call on her walkie to the person on the other end who wasn't even listening?

Yeah, that'd work great.

"Nah," the blond man said, "Didn't have much luck, if we're honest." He nodded in the direction of the injured man. "He's a bit of a lummox. Probably the reason he got shot, most likely."

On instinct, Violet looked back in the direction of the injured man, saw that he was sleeping—or *pretending* to sleep still. She turned back to the blond man and the black-haired man, they were ambling along, headed for the door to the lodge.

"Well," the blond man said, sticking his pipe between his lips once more, and zipping up his hunting jacket. "Gonna go out and check on the camp, it's not far from here, left a whole bunch of food out and wouldn't want something big and nasty to come by and swipe it."

Though Violet didn't buy, not for one second, the man's claim—not after what she'd heard from the injured man—she allowed it to go unchallenged. After all, she had no idea what these men were capable of, and so she had to play it safe.

Allow them the chance to underestimate her.

As the blond man shifted out through the front door to the lodge, he held up his hand in a sort of ragged goodbye, and then, him and the black-haired man disappeared from sight.

Violet moved quickly, keeping the walkie-talkie down at her side the whole time. She shut the door quietly behind the two men, and then she headed back over to the injured man. She tapped him on the shoulder.

He cracked an eyelid, looked at her with those swimming eyes of his. "Get out!" he said, his voice straining to achieve something above a whisper.

"Wait, why?" she said.

"Just *get out!*" he repeated, and this time his voice cracked.

"Why don't you tell me why first, huh?"

The man just continued to lie there, on the floor.

Violet caught a strong whiff of blood mixed in with antiseptic, and it made her skin crawl. She could really do with a good, strong coffee to knock the unpleasant taste out of her. She kept her attention fixed on the man. "What do they want—what're they going to do?"

The man squeezed his eyes shut and then opened them wide. "They want something," he said, his chest straining to fill with enough air. "Something . . . something I *hid* out here."

"What?" Violet said.

The man shook his head. "Not important . . . but you've gotta . . . you've gotta . . ."

Again his strength failed him. He simply couldn't get out any more words, but Violet had to know the whole thing, had to find a way to fix this situation. "Look," she said, "if you're in trouble then I can go by foot to the next lodge over—I'll get a helicopter scrambled from there." She held up her walkie-talkie so that he could see it. "Nobody's answering from the main lodge so guess I'll have to do it myself."

The man was shaking his head again. He pressed his lips tight together, so tight that all the blood left them, and then he said, "They shot him."

"Shot who?" Violet said, though, with a tightening of her gut, and a chilling of her blood, she thought that she had a fair idea.

"The warden, at the . . . at the *lodge*," he said.

Violet held herself very still. She was afraid to move now, and yet, at the same time, she knew that she had to get moving. That she was in grave danger.

This couldn't be happening to her, though.

She thought of all the time she'd spent here, in the lodge, in the middle of the woods, and she hadn't seen so much as a soul pass by.

And now this.

She had one more question on her mind, and so she asked it, "They shoot you?"

The man held still for a long time, his eyes set on hers, and then he gave a nod. "Made a . . . made a . . . wanted to send a warning . . . wanted to hurry me along . . . but"—he gave her a steely smile that, Violet could tell, was some sort of an expression of the extreme pain he was in—"they hit in the . . . in the wrong place . . . huh?"

She looked down at his gunshot wound, and to the gauze which was already matted with blood, then she looked back at him. "If I go, will they kill you?"

Again, he shook his head. "They . . . they *can't* . . . wouldn't be able to find it . . . it without me."

Violet looked him hard in the eye. "So, I have to run —run *where?*"

The man swallowed hard, and she could see that his eyes had glazed over a little.

It made Violet remember how she'd seen her mother as she'd been in the final stages of her cancer—her last days on Earth. That was the sort of pain that this man was in right now. She wanted to stay, to help him, and yet, at the same time, he was the one telling *her* that she was in danger.

"They'll kill you . . ." he said, his words drifting off as his strength failed him.

"I'll . . . I'll run," Violet finally said, getting to her feet.

The man gave her another one of those hardy grins, but when he spoke again, it was more like a sob. "No," he said. "It's too late . . . they're . . . they're back."

And, as if to confirm this observation, a bullet whizzed past Violet's ear.

4

ON GUT INSTINCT, Violet hit the floor. She could feel the tip of her ear burning, and she could feel a warmth flowing down the side of her head. Somehow she knew, without having to lift her hand up to the side of her head, that they'd shot off the top of her ear.

What surprised her all the more was how she made peace with that fact soon after it'd happened, and how she had the presence of mind to roll out of the way.

She looked up, glanced about the lodge, and knew her best chance of escape was out through the back door.

She rocked herself up onto her feet, launched herself at the door. Before she pressed down on the handle, she reached out for the pair of wire cutters which hung off a hook on the wall. She had a feeling she'd need them.

As she slipped quietly out of the back door, she heard the two men speaking.

". . . You almost fucking shot him."

It was the blond-haired man.

The black-haired man uttered a quiet apology.

Violet brought the back door shut quietly behind her, and she crouched down against the back wall of the lodge. The walls of the lodge didn't hold any of the sounds back. She could hear everything the two men were saying.

She also speculated about how, if the men were real professionals, one of them would've covered the back end of the lodge, while the other went in through the front door.

All of this added up to Violet—in her limited experience of this type of deal—as a pair of amateurs who'd somehow stumbled upon what might prove to be a great payday.

As Violet crouched down, behind the lodge, she listened into the men speaking with the injured man lying on the wooden floorboards of the living space. They were interrogating him, asking him where she'd got to.

Violet kept herself still as possible, those wire cutters still squeezed in her hand. She wondered just what she'd imagined she'd do with the wire cutters. Had she imagined that she would somehow be able to stab one or both of the men with the nose the cutters?

. . . Yeah, what *planet* was she on?

She tried to calm herself, attempted to put the fact that she was sweating all over, that her palms were dripping, out of her mind. But that was easier thought than done.

She glanced around, looked to the foliage about her, the fallen pine needles, and then to the generator, which trundled away. That was when a thought struck her.

Keeping herself crouched down, the wire cutters squeezed in her grip, she strode her way over to the cable which ran from the generator to the lodge. And then, not thinking much else, she fitted the cable between the teeth of the cutters and pressed down.

With a single, neat *snip*, the cable sprang apart.

All the lights within the lodge descended into darkness.

One of the men called out.

She listened to the other one telling him to be quiet.

Violet kept moving on her way. She knew that sooner or later, now that she'd cut the lights inside the lodge, the men's eyes would begin to adapt to the darkness. She only had a brief window of opportunity, and she had to make the most of it.

The only real advantage she had over these men with guns was the fact that, in the darkness, she knew this lodge far better than they did.

She kept herself flush against the side of the lodge, telling herself to take care with where she was putting her feet. A pine cone here, or there, would be enough to give her away.

As she headed along, a plan formed in her mind.

A *crazy* plan.

But she really couldn't see that there was any other way—no other way that a woman, out here, *unarmed*, would be able to deal with this threat.

She kept herself moving along, through the darkness, keeping her feet light as she could consciously keep them.

When she reached the trees, about twenty paces away from the lodge, she crouched down in the foliage and looked back. The lodge now was only a shape in the darkness—the only light coming from the battery-powered emergency light which hung up above the porch.

She scanned the façade for any sort of sign of something the men might've left behind, something which might help her out.

Then she saw it.

The pipe. Lying on the wooden plank of the porch.

She guessed, in the rush, when the men had seen her speaking with the injured man, that the blond man had dropped it down there. She could see that the tobacco had spilled out from it into a little pile on the wood.

But what interested her more was the match which lay beside it.

Again she moved quickly, through the darkness, keeping her body flat, and out of the dim glare of the emergency light at the porch.

When she reached the side of the lodge once more, she pressed herself up against it.

She could hear the men speaking inside—*arguing*—and she knew that she would never have a better chance.

She swiped the match off the porch, and then backtracked, headed around the lodge to the gas canister she used to cook with. She tugged the rubber tube free from the slot it was inserted into in the wall. Then she lugged it along behind her as she made her way back towards the trees where she'd been hiding out till only a couple of moments earlier.

Or several *thousand* heartbeats earlier.

It was the moment that she'd set herself down, managed to crouch down, that she heard one of the men shout out, and then, a second later, a bullet bit into the trunk of the tree just behind her. Violet ducked, still clutching hold of the match and the rubber tube which ran from the gas canister. That sulphuric scent wound through the air, and she knew that there was no other way . . . as much as it pained her to do it this was a matter of survival.

Life or death.

And so she scrubbed the match a half dozen times along the tree trunk beside her, finally getting the flicker of a flame. She hesitated a second—perhaps *two*—and then she held the flame to the rubber tube.

And with a *whompf!* she watched on as the flame danced its way along the rubber tube.

There was a brief pause when the fire reached the gas canister.

And then, with the presence of mind to hurl herself over to one side, Violet dived behind the nearest tree.

With an impossibly enormous explosion, the lodge went up in flames.

For a quick second, she was certain that she heard screams.

Perhaps all three of the men shouting out.

A couple of moments later, there was only the sound of the crackling flames.

The sight of seemingly hundreds of pieces of broken wood scattered around.

All of them quietly burning themselves out.

Violet kept herself still. She lay on her front. Staring through the grass.

She was watching for some movement—*any movement.*

But there was nothing.

They were dead.

All three of them.

She had killed them.

And, as the fact sunk in with her, she couldn't help hunching her knees up to her chest and sobbing her eyes out.

But there had been no choice.

No other way out.

They had to burn.

VOICES FROM THE CORNICE

1

EDMUND STANFORTH strutted up to the main desk of the Hilberthrudge Royale and laid his palm flat on the counter. The marble was chilled and seemed to carry a slight coating of damp . . . or *perspiration*. A rotten, woody smell seemed to hang about the whole place, like a blanket left for the winter in a log cabin by a lake.

He felt that pang, that *urge*, to urinate come at him strong again, and he jigged from one foot to the other as he looked about the lobby for someone—for *any*one. Though he could see no one about to ask, to enquire as to the whereabouts of the receptionist to the hotel, he did spot a sign which read, 'Washrooms' and he stumbled blindly across the well-polished porcelain tiles of the lobby to the entrance.

A pair of candles, stuck in odd-looking, bird-carved, wooden holders, with the candlewax dribbling down both. When he glanced down he saw that there was a puddle of wax forming there, and it seemed to have been forming for some time, given its size and circumference.

Edmund felt the warm glow off the candles, and he imagined it magnified several thousand times in his mind, given the snowy weather outside, the weather he'd come through, and the several dozen times his car had almost slid right off the road while making his way up this hill.

When the manager of the hotel finally made an appearance, Edmund swore that he'd make it a matter of great urgency to enquire as to why the roads hadn't been properly salted in preparation for this weather.

Then again, this place, this *hotel*, was quite a long way from any true civilisation and, as such, Edmund speculated that such modern innovations had yet to pass through their Neanderthal brains.

He strutted up to the door which was marked 'Gentlemen' in peeling golden lettering. He reached down, for the wooden handle of the door, and turned it.

The handle remained stuck, unmovable.

Another pang, another warm *surge* passed through his bladder, and he knew that he couldn't hold on for much longer. And what kind of place did this hotel think it was to lock the toilets down in the lobby? Did they get many passing travellers so desperate for the toilet that they mounted a charge up the twisting mountain road Edmund had just travelled along, to make it necessary to lock the door?

Then he looked over to the door marked 'Ladies' and, still seeing nobody about, he tried that door handle too.

Just as locked as the first.

"Ahh!" Edmund couldn't resist blurting out, and throwing up his hands as he did so.

He glanced back over his shoulder, back to the main desk of the hotel, wondering whether someone might've slunk up behind the desk while he'd been investigating the toilets.

Nope.

He eyed both the toilet doors and the thought momentarily crossed his mind that he might find some blunt object, some fire extinguisher or, knowing this place, some moose head hanging off the wall as a 'trophy.'

But doing something so rash would only get him on the wrong side of the village police force, wherever they might be located, and from Edmund's 'delightful' previous experiences of these bumpkin-filled backwaters, that was an awfully poor idea.

It could get him locked up for days even, till they got one of the lawyers back in the city to come out here and clear matters up. To inform them that Edmund Stanforth was in fact an executive director of one of the largest financial institutions in the country: Eastern Investments. In fact, as Edmund's metaphorical lawyer would swear, this very hotel had most likely partaken of some form of loan, or other financial service of Edmund's institution, sometime in their past.

And so *who* were they to stand in his way?

Who were they to lock up their toilets and leave the reception desk unstaffed?

Who, indeed, and Edmund resolved, as he danced from one foot to the other, that he would see this manager, whoever he might be, eye to eye, or else there would be fireworks.

And these bumpkins sure wouldn't like to see fireworks.

———

Edmund returned to the lobby lounge, where he took in the décor of the place. It was what he would've termed flypaper chic, at least he would've if he hadn't been so desperate for a piss. The wallpaper looked like all his memories of his grandmother's wardrobe of dresses all combined in dizzying and ugly, faded patterns. And the half dozen armchairs more or less scattered about the place in random fashion looked as if they'd long stood neglected.

Dust just seemed to puff up from all over the place, forming clouds, getting up his nostrils, and smothering the back of his throat. He knew that even just having been in this place for a matter of minutes that he'd need to take a hearty shower to get himself anywhere near what he was satisfied with branding 'clean.'

He walked the wooden-planked floor, hearing the planks give and *groan* beneath his weight. He supposed this place must be ripe with wood rot, along with just about any other sort of rot that was going.

He approached the main desk again, and spotted the brass bell which he hadn't noticed before. It might've been because the bell was so thick with dust, so dulled from the thin trickle of light that glowed from the light bulb above the desk, that he had mistaken it for a hairball the no-doubt resident flea-bag cat had deposited there.

Edmund dipped into the pocket of his jacket and produced the handkerchief that he kept there for unpleasant tasks such as this one. And even with the buffer of the handkerchief, he couldn't help but clasp his eyes shut as he reached across the desk and gave the plunger of the bell a tentative jab.

Ding!

Well, at least the bell's chime didn't seem much affected by the rest of its state, or the state of its surroundings. And Edmund sat back on his heels, trying his best to push that overwhelming urge to piss to the back of his mind.

Someone would be along shortly. *Surely* they would.

He glanced back over his shoulder, looked out through the large glass doors to the cracked concrete of the car park and he wondered if he might be better off going *au naturel*. But, then again, the thought of the local police played on his mind.

He was in no doubt that every backwater bumpkin was out to get him somehow. And a swift charge of public urination, or whatever the hell the law said, would be just the ticket for them.

People like this, people who ran places like this, they were nothing less than scum.

Pure human *scum*.

He waited and waited, feeling his heart ticking on and the blood trickling about his veins. He had reached the point now where he could hardly dare to move for fear that he might release his bladder. And since he hadn't pissed himself since he'd been a six-year-old, he was quite keen to keep his streak going.

By the time the shallow echo of the bell had resonated back

into silence, he thought of giving it another go. But he couldn't quite summon the will, to bring his handkerchief out again, to *touch* the damn, dusty thing once more.

And so he settled on a simple bellow.

"Hello! Is there anyone *here?*"

He listened to his voice echo about the lobby and, he hoped, through every corridor, every bedroom, of the place. That might get someone's attention. Get someone to actually give him some service here.

But, most importantly, get someone to unlock the bloody doors to the toilets so he didn't have to dance from foot to foot like some idiot schoolchild.

Just as with the bell, he listened to the echo of his voice cease, and realised that there was no response forthcoming.

Some people.

Did they even understand they were in the service industry?

Sometimes it was impossible to tell . . .

He gave it another go. "Anyone *fucking* awake here at all?! Or am I just standing here all on my own? Self-service, I take it!"

Again, he listened to his voice echo about the place, ebb in and out of the corridors upstairs, and then he let loose a hard and jagged sigh.

He dipped his hand into his pocket and withdrew his mobile phone. He flipped through the screens, got up his personal assistant's number, and then punched out a quick email, detailing the address of the hotel, the name: Hilberthrudge Royale, and then the complaint that he wished his assistant to make on his behalf.

That was the problem with the world—the *service* industry in particular. There was so much complaining to be done that a busy man, like himself, could quite easily forget. Have the whole thing slip his mind. Let the bastards off scot-free.

Message sent, he thought about bellowing again, but, just as he was on the point of doing so, he heard a whisper . . . well, actually, more like a chill really, running about the collar of his shirt. And he glanced off to his side, almost certain someone was standing at his shoulder.

He spun about.

No one there.

He felt the same chill running about his neck, and he brought his hand up to touch the chill, to feel it layering on against his skin.

Weird, really weird. But he'd spent so much time on the road, and he had to piss so badly now that he didn't have time to worry about something as extraneous as a draught. A place like this, a place like the Hilberthrudge Royale, well it just about demanded that draughts would *have* to be present in some way.

But this was odder than a normal draught because it wasn't billowing up all around him, like all the draughts which he'd experienced thus far in his life had tended to do. No, it appeared to be blowing in at him from a specific direction, almost as if someone—someone with a razor-like chill to their breath—was blowing against him.

And, since there was no one about, he assumed that this theoretical person would also need to be invisible.

He peered off across the lobby, over to a pair of those ugly, battered armchairs sitting beside the open fire, now only crackling away dimly, its embers almost died out from lack of attention. And then his eyes fell to the mantelpiece, and then to the decorative swirls that adorned it there.

Funny, it seemed to Edmund just about the only aspect of the hotel that had *any* class. That mantelpiece, those swirls on the cornice. It seemed so out of place compared to the rest of the décor, so much so that it made him immediately suspicious, made him reach the conclusion that, perhaps, this place, this hotel, had once been a much grander location before the current proprietor had moved in . . . and brought their hideous taste, and lacking hygiene habits, to bear on the place.

For a moment, feeling that fire-hot urge to piss disintegrate just a cinch, he picked his way back across the floorboards, and over to the two armchairs beside the fire.

2

A S EDMUND GOT CLOSER to the fireplace, closer to the mantelpiece that hung over it, he felt the hairs all over his body begin to rise, and his heart quicken its beat. Something about this, something about this . . . this *cornice* was odd to him. It struck a chord, drew on some sort of memory, something that he couldn't place from his past.

And he was quite sure now that it was here the draught was coming from.

He stepped closer to the cornice, now feeling that swirl of chilly air blow up against his cheeks, blow against his slickly gelled-back hair, and send that swilling feeling down through his gut. His mouth was dry and he could really do with a beer, though, already having acquainted himself with this place, he doubted very much they had a *functional* bar of their own.

Most likely the nearest bar to this place would be back down the road, in that town he'd passed through. What had it been called? He scoured his mind a few moments, and then recalled.

Yes, Sesney, that was it.

Another *backwards*-sounding place name.

The draught from the cornice continued to blow against his face, and he reached out, sure that the draught must in fact be coming from the fireplace, and somehow swilling its way down from there, a trick of the senses.

He reached forwards, his fingers rigid and his heart bobbling against his ribs, and he felt the draught get stronger, felt it get chillier, and his blood get cold along with it.

His fingers were only inches from the cornice itself when it got so cold that he couldn't bear bringing his skin any closer to the chilly draught, and he drew them back, pouted to himself, and then straightened up, wondering just what the hell that was all about.

Most likely he was just tired, *tired* and hungry, and in need of a drink.

And, good God, a *piss*.

Just as he stared on at the cornice, still feeling that swill of cold air blow against his skin, he heard a quiet voice, almost imperceptibly close to his ear.

". . . Hello?"

He spun round, checked over his shoulder, no one there at all. Just the armchairs all sitting about the lobby, and the deserted front desk. Through the windows he could just about see out into the car park, to his car slotted into its space, the sole vehicle parked up in the place.

Edmund felt a scowl forming on his face, and he took no steps to prevent its formation. He let it grow there. While he was certain that what he'd just heard had simply been a figment of his imagination, that he'd just been hearing something in his mind, it had hardly helped to lighten his already dim view of the Hilberthrudge Royale.

Not only was this place a mess, service-wise, but it was also beginning to make him feel uncomfortable. Edmund was used to the city, to the roads jammed full with cars, and the people jostling on the pavement to get to work . . . or at least that was what he would see from the backseat of his chauffeur-driven car.

He *knew* that he should've insisted a little harder on a chauffeur for this trip. At least now he wouldn't have been alone in this incredibly odd place, this bumpkin's manor house, or whatever the hell it was.

"Sir?"

Edmund spun around again, looked to the front desk, the direction from where the voice had come from.

Praises be offered to the gods, finally someone had turned up!

Edmund turned away from the fireplace, and broke into a stodgy march, headed right on a collision course with the front desk.

———

At the front desk was a young man, perhaps in his early twenties, with cropped blond hair and wearing a crisp, neat suit with, what Edmund was sure to be, a velvet tie.

The young man smiled at Edmund, a few laughter lines breaking out around his eyes as he did so. And that only served to wind Edmund up all the more, because if there was one thing he couldn't stand aside from *poor* service, it was the bloody-mindedness to try and pass it off with something so simple as a smile.

Edmund gave the young man a scowl for his troubles. He guessed this young man to be about the same age as his son, Henry.

Now, if Henry had ever worked in a place like this—God forbid!—he would've been appalled to know that he'd left a guest, a *customer*, waiting at the front desk, while he was doing whatever he had been doing out back.

Mercifully for Henry, he'd never had to lower himself to doing such jobs, never had to take these lower-class jobs. He'd fixed it so that Henry got a decent entry-level position in his financial institution. Nothing with *real* responsibility, of course, though Edmund often flirted with the idea of promoting Henry sooner or later. It was almost Christmas, after all, and he had always nurtured that image of father and son striding out side to side, doing battle with business connections, sealing the deal together.

In his mind, he had rehearsed that celebratory high-five perhaps one too many times.

But that didn't make him any less determined to make it come true.

Yes, he would do just that, when Henry got back from his holiday in the Caribbean, they'd settle it all then.

With warm thoughts of his son on his mind, Edmund turned back to the lobby boy. "Where the *hell* were you?" he said.

The young man kept up that same, *infuriating*, smile, then said, "I'm sorry, sir, I guess I didn't hear the bell at all. This is low-season, see? Don't get all that many guests."

Edmund rolled his eyes, and then slapped his hand down on that marble counter. He was greatly annoyed that this didn't make the young man so much as flinch. His ability to intimidate was just about the most valuable tool in his arsenal when it came to standing up for his consumer comforts.

"I've been bellowing my lungs out for half an age out here." Then, feeling that familiar heat rise through his bladder, he added, "And where the *hell* do you get off in locking up the toilets, eh? What's the whole idea behind that?"

The young man kept up his easy smile and then ducked down behind the counter. He scrabbled around down there, out of sight, and Edmund heard an awful lot of tinkling, and caught a whiff of that unmistakable scent of brass . . . or whatever the hell they made keys with.

When the young man popped back up, he held a ring of keys tight in his fist. "I'm sorry, sir, it must've skipped my mind, this is low-season after all."

Edmund sneered long and hard, and then lurched over the counter and snatched the keys out of the young man's hand. As he beat a retreat for the toilets, already feeling the urge to piss almost overwhelming him, almost able to smell the *stink* of piss in his nostrils, he said, over his shoulder, "Yeah, you said that already. Low-season or not, this is a flea-bitten, sorry-state of a hotel."

3

EDMUND STANFORTH finally arrived in his room, a room snuggled away up on the fifth floor of the Hilberthrudge Royale and even in his scrabble for the light switch, he was already certain he wasn't going to like what he saw.

Snap! went the light switch when he eventually found it, and a sallow light radiated out from the dusty, old bulb that looked, to Edmund, as if it'd been fitted sometime around Time Immemorial.

Still, not much else to do about it now. He could hardly spend the night out in his car, though its cleanliness was extremely attractive. He'd caught a glance at an arcane thermometer down in the lobby and seen the outside temperature had dipped below minus five. And though he hadn't much concerns about money, in running the car engine all night with the heater going like the dickens, he was more worried about finding a petrol station in the morning.

No doubt even if there *was* so much as a petrol station down in the village at the base of the hill—back in *Sesney*—then most likely the second the bumpkins that ran the place saw his sleek sports car they'd claim they'd simply run out of petrol altogether.

God, he hated the countryside.

He stepped over those still-creaking floorboards and to the poorly-made bed. The sheets were a kind of sludge-brown colour with a mulch-green blanket draped over the top of the affair. And he could see all the lint hanging off the bedspread that revealed the bedding to be at least into its second decade, if not its third.

How these people survived in business really got his goat.

Though, he supposed, supply and demand was truly a golden goose out here in this backwater.

That sour, watery smell hung about this bedroom too, just as it had down in the lobby, and that woody scent at the back everything, the one that got to the back of his throat, and reminded him of how a sauna smelled.

He pressed his hand to the bed and listened to the springs creak long and hard and, even after he withdrew his hand, they went on creaking to themselves like a gander of old country maids bringing in baskets of laundry from the creek out back.

He let loose a long-held sigh, and then glanced about the room, just looking for something else that might give him some reason for optimism ahead of his night's stay . . . other than the finite nature of night itself.

He noticed an old-style television, complete with its concave screen and, of course, the Hilberthrudge Royale's trademarked mounted dust hanging onto it for dear life. The thing actually had a remote control—an *actual remote control*—goodness knew what other wonders this place might have in store for Edmund.

A couple of paintings hung up on the walls too. Those kinds of washed-out oil paintings that'd been all the rage around the turn of the century. The turn of the *twentieth* century.

And the less said about the drapes, the better.

But 'mould' was the operative word of any superficial description.

Well, Edmund had stayed in worse places, although it was something of a struggle to think of one right at the moment. But he supposed he'd just have to make the best of it. He calmed himself somewhat by reassuring himself that his personal assistant would be getting on with those letters of complaint, perhaps even getting a lawyer's letter drafted—bless her cotton socks—to send to the manager of the hotel.

Because, goodness knew, Edmund was far too weary to bother trying to drive the man out of whatever rat hole he'd tucked himself into right at that moment in time.

And so he threw off his neat pair of smart-casual trainers, draped his jacket over the back of the rickety looking wicker chair and then threw himself down onto the bed, clicking off the light switch as he descended.

He slipped off to sleep with the creaking and jerking of those springs loud in his thoughts, and he thought of places long and far away.

————

Edmund woke up with a chilly draught working its way across his face. When he reached up to touch his forehead he realised that he was sweating profusely. He raised himself up onto his side, using his elbows to do so, and he blinked out into the gloom which seemed to press down on him from all sides.

He blinked again, realised just where he was, and felt a slight pang at the pit of his stomach. Hunger? Possibly.

He had been having the strangest dream, a deeply odd, quite disturbing dream. He thought back over it, tried to scrabble for some remainder—some illustrative fragment—but came up empty handed. He never could remember dreams, nor did he waste his time fawning over their meanings, which was less than he could say for some of his partners.

They thought that being an executive gave them some sort of a visionary quality, as if they were more than just a business*man* . . . or woman, since this was the modern age, after all . . . and he'd sat through more coffee mornings than he cared to count where some partner or other had talked about the significance of the flamingos, or the palomino pony, or the *dwarf*—what was it with *dwarves* in people's dreams?—until Edmund was just about ready to slip the tie off from around his neck, turn it into a knot and then pummel to death whoever happened to be relating said dream.

Just thinking about it got him irate. He squeezed his fingers into fists and felt his fingernails bury into the palms of his hands. There. A little pain. Sometimes that went a long way to getting you sharper. Sometimes as good as a slung-back shot of espresso.

He blinked a little more, and then stretched long and hard. Then he gave a yawn and rocked himself to his feet. He glanced to the ivory-coloured, plastic phone which stood on his bedside table and, with another blink, he remembered just what sort of a place the Hilberthrudge Royale was. And how, even in high-season, he'd have been a little optimistic to have wished for something so opulent as twenty-four-hour room service.

An international player, the Hilberthrudge Royale would never be.

And after his experience here, with all the fury and hellfire he could rustle up, he would make that a certainty.

Whenever he did wake up in the middle of the night in a hotel, a frequent occurrence while he was on the road, he would usually order room service, and then go for a little walk.

Sometimes, in the better places that Edmund stayed, the hotel had a garden, complete with pleasant tinkling fountains, and rich-smelling roses. Sometimes they even had the bright idea of plonking a swimming pool right in the middle of it all. And just a quick tip to the midnight porter, or whoever happened to be on duty, would see him being allowed to take a dip in the pool too: opening hours be damned.

Edmund held out no such hopes for the Hilberthrudge Royale, but he knew that he couldn't suffer lying on that bed, on those dank-smelling and moist blankets while those springs beneath him scratched out some cacophony or other—like some 'arty' orchestra—while he waited for the sandman to come calling on him.

No, because he had experienced so many years of his insomnia to have become intimately familiar with its patterns, to learn them well and to know them better than the rhythm of his own heartbeat.

But at least he might be permitted to take his walk.

4

OUT ON THE FIFTH-FLOOR CORRIDOR, Edmund let loose another unwieldy yawn, which he just about stifled with his hand, though there was no one about to see. He guessed that manners were something that was conditioned, rather than learned.

His heart thudded gently, the only sound in his otherwise muted hearing, and he felt the same-old chill of that draught eking its way along the corridor, rising up the hairs all over his body. Keeping him bright-eyed awake.

When he reached the end of the fifth-floor corridor, he descended the spiral staircase, the same one which the lobby boy had shown him up just hours before, and, as Edmund recalled with clarity, he'd suggested that perhaps—just *perhaps*—since this was the 'low-season' after all, that the lobby boy might show him to a room on a lower floor.

The lobby boy had simply smirked at him—*smirked!*—as if this was some sort of a joke, but then, when he'd read the expression off Edmund's face, he'd soon seen sense, and explained that during the 'low-season' only the rooms on the top floor of the hotel were kept prepared for guests.

It was a question of heating, apparently, based on the manager of the hotel's presumption that hot air always rose, and formed the basis of a cost-cutting masterstroke.

Edmund had been in business long enough to know that complaints to simple working hands did no good, and so he'd kept his business acumen to himself, though he'd also reminded himself to have that particular complaint added to his letter—the letter his personal assistant had hopefully got all drafted and posted to Edmund's inbox, ready for him to inject any necessary snappy turns of bile where they needed injecting.

As Edmund descended the spiral staircase, he gripped the banister, and only then did he truly realise, in the moonlight which streamed in through the long window, that the banister itself was carved out of mahogany, and well-polished, too.

Just as with that cornice he'd noticed earlier on, down in the lobby, the foundations of the Hilberthrudge Royale were undoubtedly solid, extremely well-founded. And he could see, as if his eyes extended the vision to form before him, how the place might've looked if sufficient care had been placed in the selection of the décor.

The whole place seemed a graveyard of potential.

Did it just need a necromancer?

Edmund pommelled on down the thin carpet of the staircase, and he gripped on tight to the banister, still feeling sleep holding him in its midnight embrace. He didn't quite have the capacities of the daytime restored to his senses just yet. But give it a few hours. It was funny the strength sunlight could give him.

He kept on winding his way down that spiral staircase, counting off the deserted floors as he went, breathing in the rising dust as he kicked it up from the carpets. Good thing he'd never had allergies. He'd never been one of *those* children at school. He had always been big, and healthy, captain of the rugby team, the football team, the cricket team.

A *competitor*.

He wound on down, plunging deeper, closer to the lobby of the Hilberthrudge Royale, and he felt his lungs sucking the air in and then plonking it back out again before him. His heartbeat stayed steady and that gentle layer of perspiration continued to dampen his skin.

And that *infernal* draught just kept scuttling about, lingering over his skin, keeping him chilled as a refrigerated cut of meat.

He reached the lobby, deserted, of course. Good thing really that he hadn't bothered with the telephone, he might've disturbed the lobby boy's beauty sleep, and that truly would've been a pity. No, the lobby looked just as it had when he'd entered earlier in the day, except that whereas before that light bulb had glowed above the reception desk, now it was the moonlight that provided the only scrap of light about the place.

Edmund sighed hard, and then his eyes fell across a deserted bar standing off to the other side of the lobby. A pleasant surprise. And unmanned. He glanced about him, though really had no idea why. Had he been checking for security cameras? No, most likely something inside him had been jabbing at him to check for any bumpkin that might be skulking about in the shadows, ready to bring the local police to bear on this *outsider*.

Because, everything else considered, this night spent—*wasted* —in the Hilberthrudge Royale, he knew that he wouldn't permit himself to be made a slave of these countryside people. Tomorrow he would pay his bill, send his letter of complaint, and be on his way to his destination. And he would think no more about this place, other than to rub Sesney off his satellite navigation system or . . . better . . . daub it with a red dot so that he could avoid it in the future.

He trod up to the bar, took another glance about, then ducked under the counter. He busied himself looking over the glass cases, at the bottles all nestled inside. It looked like a nice, strong whisky might do the trick, might get him back off to sleep if he was lucky.

Get him *out* of this place all the quicker.

And the cabinet wasn't locked either.

He snatched the bottle out, unscrewed it and then poured himself a couple of fingers into a—surprisingly—undusty tumble. He rolled the liquid at the bottom of the glass half a dozen times, brought it up for a sniff.

Pure malty goodness.

Then he sucked the stuff back, wincing a little as that hot bite hit the back of his throat, and then proceeded to burn him all the way down.

"Ahh!" he got out, into the empty lobby, shaking his head.

He glanced about himself suspiciously, as if someone might've heard him raiding the Hilberthrudge Royale's drinks cabinet. But, just like before, there was no one about.

So he poured himself another glass and then made his way over to the fireplace, to those pair of armchairs standing there, their backs to him.

He sat in one, and gazed off into the sooty remnants of what had been the fire before there. He could still catch a few waves of its residual warmth, and it seemed to extend the warmth from the whisky he felt in his chest, dragging it out of him, expanding it.

Perhaps this wasn't such a bad place after all.

One thing that whisky hadn't taken care of, however, was that chilly draught that just seemed to pervade the whole damn hotel. And here it was just as bad as it had been up on the fifth floor. In fact, worse.

He felt that stiff torrent of the draught coming at him direct, and when he looked up, to the cornice above the fireplace, he realised just where it was coming from.

He swivelled out of his chair, already feeling the alcohol burying him deep into those mottled, squidged-up cushions, and he rocked back onto his feet, approached the cornice tentatively.

Sure now that the draught was coming from the cornice, he reached out his hand, and felt the draught lick about his hand, bathe it in the cool breeze.

Where was it coming from?

He inspected the cornice closer in the moonlight, and he could see no hole there. He reached out to touch it, found it cool, plaster. Smooth. He brought his hand back and took another sip of his whisky.

This time, however, even as he felt the warmth from the whisky burrowing down through him, he felt the chill take precedence. By far stronger than the draught could possibly be.

Or than he could have possibly thought.

And then he heard the voice, light as the draught, in his ear.

Distinct. Clear words. A voice.

A *man's* voice.

". . . Hello?"

Edmund stumbled back, fell into the armchair, and he felt the glass of whisky slip from between his fingers and fall to the solid wooden floor, smashing into a thousand pieces at his feet.

5

F OR LONG MOMENTS, stretched out in his mind, Edmund scrabbled about, his arms lashing at the air as if someone might be trying to restrain him. Then he realised that it was all in his mind. Just a trick of his mind.

He'd heard a voice, sure he had.

And, look, right over there, that trophy mounted on that wall, that was a unicorn's head, wasn't it?

He stabilised himself in the chair, and shoved himself to the edge of its battered, old cushion, perching on it. He stared for a long time at the cornice, as if it might be about to swivel out from its place, spin through the air and gouge his eyes out.

Of course it stayed put.

In the moonlight streaming in through the windows of the lobby, Edmund caught the reflection of the shards from the smashed glass of whisky all about him. He swore under his breath and then crouched down, beginning to gather them up, to lay them out in his palm.

Just his luck. Just when he'd thought he'd found a little, teensy, tiny scrap of consolation about the Hilberthrudge Royale, and look what had happened . . .

Nah, this place was a shitball, nothing less.

Just like he'd pinned it from the start.

He had got up most of the shards of glass when he heard the creak of floorboards, off to the other side of the lobby. He held still, blood freezing in his veins, and every muscle seeming to lock up. He attempted to peel back the night with his eyes, but could only make out the vague gloom in the half-light dribbling into the lobby from the moon.

"Anyone there?" Edmund said, his voice sounding much

frailer than he'd intended, much weaker and less substantial than he ever made a point of it sounding in company.

As if in anticipation of this detail, he gave a little cough and then swallowed hard.

The floorboards creaked on, and Edmund glanced back over his shoulder, now sure that was the direction the sound was coming from. But all he could see was the darkness, thick and unwavering.

"Hello?" he said again, this time sounding more confident.

Another creak of the floorboard and then someone spoke. A warm voice, a kind voice. Deep. One which immediately sent a shudder running up Edmund's spine, made him feel like a small child who'd snuck downstairs afterhours.

"Good Evening"—the man paused a moment—"or perhaps I should say, Good Morning."

Edmund remembered himself, just where he was, what he'd been doing. He found his feet, still conscious of the broken glass all gathered in the palm of his hand, and the smell of whisky which now lingered in the air between them.

Even now, in the darkness with this stranger, he had the urge to have another drink. Another whisky. Just to put the devil back in his hole, to get him back to sleep. A long time ago he had given up drinking to get to sleep, but this case, being here, in the Hilberthrudge Royale, well that required drastic measures.

"Yes," Edmund said, replying to the stranger, "Good Morning, I . . . uh, I mean, I wasn't able to sleep, and so—"

"And so you've come down here to raid my whisky cabinet?"

Edmund felt his insides cool, and a pang in his chest. He hated being caught off guard, unprepared. He had been so sure that he'd remain unbothered down here, in this lobby. And now he was standing here, in the darkness, with a stranger. A man who he could not see . . . though he was sure that, just within the gloom, he could make out a vague shape.

Edmund realised, several seconds too late, that the tone of the stranger's voice, his question, had been meant as a kind of joke. And so he laughed hollowly, feeling the laughter jab his ribs into his lungs, kneed the air out of him.

"Yes," Edmund said, feeling on sturdier ground now, "I *am* sorry. You see, I was having some trouble sleeping and so I took to taking a walk, and then I saw the drinks cabinet down here and thought it might just be a good way to sweep me off to dreamland."

He hesitated a moment, remarking on how the darkness, how this speaking to an invisible stranger had robbed him of his previous cocksureness. And, he realised, it was because he was at a disadvantage. "I was always going to pay, of course, when I check out in the morning."

"Where are you travelling to?"

"Oh, hmm? . . . Ah, just business, nothing interesting I'm afraid, just the normal thing, really. Come out here to see to a client—a very *important* client." Then Edmund decided that he'd had enough of playing the fool, and that now was as good a time as any to reveal just who his conversational companion really was. "Uh, you couldn't flip on the lights, could you? I, uh, couldn't find them on my way down here."

For a moment Edmund was certain that stranger hadn't heard him . . . or, worse, that he had *heard* him but that he had no intention of complying with his request. But then Edmund heard the same squeaking of the floorboards, that shifting of the man's form through the darkness, and then the *snap* of the light switch, and the dim glow coming off the light bulb just above the reception desk.

Edmund took in the man, still with his back towards him for the time being. First of all he noted his skin colour. Black. Impossibly black, almost. Black as the blackest of the darkness, the darkness that had scurried off into the corners of the lobby.

And he wore a long overcoat, that same mulch-green of the blanket up on the bed upstairs, Edmund noted, and it floated right down to the heels of the man's shoes—boots?—which was no mean accomplishment considering that the man had a towering figure, and great big, broad shoulders.

Just looking at him from behind, and across the lobby from him, Edmund knew that he was easily a head and shoulders shorter than the man.

The man turned around, fixed Edmund with his stare, with those chocolate-brown eyes of his, and then he trod his way, slowly but surely, across the lobby floor, with all those accompanying creaks from the wooden planks below, towards Edmund.

Edmund stood his ground, only realising from the prick when he tried to close his hand, that he still held all those shards there from the smashed whisky glass. He glanced about him and noticed a couple of other fragments that he still hadn't collected up and, by way of prolonging further conversation, or so he reflected on later, he stooped to pick up all the remaining pieces within reach.

When he straightened up, the man stood a few paces away from him, just as large and black as he'd been when Edmund had first regarded him over at the reception desk.

"I understand you wished to speak with the manager," the man said.

Edmund felt his heart pounding away in his chest, and something akin to a flapping within his stomach, but he finally found his words, and a little of the resolve he'd had when he'd first arrived at the Hilberthrudge Royale.

"Oh, well, there were just a few things that I wanted to mention."

The man pouted slightly, but his expression didn't change otherwise, and his chocolate-brown eyes seemed just as warm as they had previously.

"Like, uh, the . . . the lobby toilets"—Edmund pointed off, a little wildly, to the corner of the lobby, to where the toilets were located—"when I arrived, you see, I was desperate, and there was no one around. And, well"—he managed a nervous smile, but it soon slipped off his lips—"well, I almost wet myself waiting."

The man made something between the sound of a moan and a grunt right from the base of his throat. That sound sent a scurry through Edmund's veins.

"And, the other thing," Edmund said, thinking quickly, and with his heart pattering the way it was, wanting to get out of this exchange as soon as possible, "my bedroom. You see, it's got damp—*mould*, in some places, and, and, uh . . ."

"This *is* low-season," the man replied.

"Ah, yes, that was just what the lobby boy told me."

"Thomas?"

"Yes, just what Thomas told me, he, uh, said that as it was low-season that it wasn't your policy to open the toilets in the lobby." With great effort, Edmund wrestled his neck upwards, to look the man in those chocolate-brown eyes again. "Is that, uh, uh, what you would confirm?"

The man made that odd grumbling sound again, at the very base of his throat, and then he said, "Mr Stanforth, what you must understand is that we do not open the Hilberthrudge Royale in low-season for just *anyone*."

"What do you mean?"

But the man only looked deep into Edmund's eyes, as if he was trying to divine some truth from something deep down inside of Edmund's soul.

6

EDMUND'S HEART pounded thickly in his ears, almost as if he was on a train, that was just what it reminded him of . . . yes, like a train thrumming through a tunnel, and his ears getting all filled up with air so that he'd have to swallow hard to restore his hearing.

That was just what it was like.

He glanced back down to those fragments of glass resting in his palm, and wondered just what should be done with them. Though it pained him to look back at the man, he managed to do so, albeit briefly, and he scuttled over the floorboards, and back to the bar, where he swept the pieces of glass off his palm and into the bin there.

Just as he was on the point of turning around, he caught a glance at the cabinet again, at the bottles all nestled inside, and he knew that he *had* to have another drink. He waited a moment, counted out a couple dozen heartbeats, then he glanced back over his shoulder and said, to the man standing there—the manager, it seemed, "Would you care for drink? My treat?"

The manager, the huge black man in the overcoat, just regarded him with those self-same, chocolate-brown eyes, and slightly inclined his head, an almost imperceptible shake.

"Well," Edmund said, eyeing the bottle, "then you won't mind if I do?" He paused again before adding, "And of course you'd add it to my bill."

The manager didn't seem to respond either negatively or positively to this proposal, and so Edmund just poured out another glass from the bottle.

As he raised his glass up to his lips, he noticed his hand shaking, and it only got worse as he drank. He felt a cool drop of whisky trickle down his chin, along with the burn at the back of his throat, and the sour malt smell filling his nostrils.

And when it got down to his stomach, the warm fuzz was almost subdued entirely from that chilling draught that blew through the lobby.

Seeing a chance for some conversation, an opportunity to defuse this fraught encounter, he turned to the manager and said, "Have you tried to do anything to prevent that draught, at all?"

The manager's face remained still, unfeeling. And Edmund thought that perhaps he hadn't heard the question. Oh sure, this man seemed a little odd, all that sneaking about in the dark, and then his *mysterious* way of speaking, but Edmund surely hadn't got the impression that he was just flat-out rude.

Though, as with anyone in the world, Edmund was prepared to revise his judgement at any point or any time.

He felt a quiver pass through his stomach, and he laid his palm flat against his gut, as if guarding against it happening again. That was the problem, he'd drunk on an empty stomach. But what other options had been available to him? The Hilberthrudge Royale had no restaurant, or, at least, it wasn't open in 'low-season.'

Edmund stared at the last dregs of his whisky, in the bottom of the glass, and then, after half-thinking of just laying the glass back down on the counter, he felt the manager's eyes heavy on him, and he decided to finish it.

That last swallow seemed to push something inside him over the edge, and the whisky caught at the back of his throat, sending a wave of boiling-hot blood rushing through his system and bile rushing up against his tongue.

He swallowed hard, and bucked his shoulders as he replaced the glass back on the bar counter. He glanced to the manager who remained in the same spot, still watching him closely. "I, uh," Edmund started, feeling more than a little giddy now, "I should head back up to my room, I think."

He began walking across the wooden floorboards, and that *creak* continued to sound. And that draught just got all the chillier, cutting him right down to the bone. As he drew level with the manager, he could hardly keep his gait steady. When the manager addressed him, Edmund couldn't avoid flinching.

"Did you see them?" he said.

Edmund wheeled about, found himself standing right before the manager, his great big bulk towering over him, and the manager's chocolate-brown eyes peering down his nose right into his. The draught got stronger, almost to the level of a breeze, Edmund could feel it blowing against his trouser leg, tussling the material up against his skin.

"I'm . . . I'm sorry, what?" Edmund finally got out.

"Did you see them, did you at least *hear* them?"

"Uh, hear *who?*" Edmund said, secretly pleased that, considering the spiralling nausea which now gripped his gut, and the way that draught seemed to cling to him like a freezing-cold, invisible claw, his voice had come out almost unwavering, almost unmoved.

"The voices," the manager said, his eyes now twitching from side to side in their sockets, as if he was picking through Edmund's bones.

"What 'voices?'"

"The ones from the cornice," the manager said, his arm raising at his side, and his finger, seemingly detached from himself, straightening out to point to the fireplace, to the cornice which remained, just as it had been before, lining the edge of the mantelpiece.

Edmund attempted a dry chuckle, but, and perhaps it was the whisky catching his voice, or maybe just that *unplaceable* draught, he choked on it again. And he tasted that same bile swilling its way up his gullet, as if toying with the idea of choking him. He discarded the idea as quickly as it struck him, of course. The very idea that his *own* body might be trying to kill him.

"I . . . I beg your pardon?" Edmund said.

The manager continued to eyeball Edmund, his eyes never leaving his, and the emotion still remaining totally absent from his face. Edmund knew, instinctively, that the manager would not repeat just what he had said, would not say it again.

And right then, right at that moment, the feeling of unease grew to be uncontrollable, and Edmund knew that he had to get out of the hotel. Right now. He couldn't stand another second in the place.

So, with a final, fleeting glance to the manager, he strode on past him, making for the spiral stairs, heading back up them to his room on the fifth floor.

7

BACK UP IN HIS BEDROOM, Edmund felt the uneasiness grow even heavier as it weighed on his mind. He scrabbled about, gathering up his wheelie suitcase which laid at the foot of his bed. He shovelled his wash bag inside, and then his mobile phone, and, finally, he plucked his car keys off the bedside table, where he'd dropped them.

As he seized hold of the handle of the suitcase, he ran through a mental checklist. Something nagged away from the corner of his mind, something telling him that he'd forgotten something. But what? What could he possibly have forgotten?

He glanced about the room, and at the same time became revolted all over again by that blanket, by the *mould* which appeared to line everything, and to the *dankness* that appeared to stick to everything. It all seemed all the more potent now, even *more* powerful. And he knew that he needed to get far away from this place. To get some fresh air. If these bumpkin local police wished to stop him out there, to breathalyse him and lock him up in the station back in Sesney, then that was just fine with him.

At least he wouldn't have to spend another moment here, in the Hilberthrudge Royale.

And that would be a fine consolation.

A fine *enough* consolation.

As he made his way to the door of his bedroom, he heard the *creak* of the floorboards out in the corridor, and he knew that the manager had followed him up the stairs, and he knew that he would be out there, in the hallway, waiting for him.

All of a sudden, Edmund felt his skin turn to jelly, and his mind race. Never before, never in his whole life, had he given in to panic, allowed it to take him over so completely as it did then. But, though he had no training, no past experience to aid him, he knew that he mustn't allow it to rule his actions. He must think pragmatically, be logical, use all those abilities which had got him into such a prized position, in such a *noble* financial institution as Eastern Investments. He was a doer—had *always* been a doer—and—*Godammit!*—he would be a doer right now.

He pressed on, and bounded for his bedroom door, determined to have the element of surprise, he would catch the man unawares, and if he tried to stop him, if he tried to grab a hold of him, why Edmund would be too quick for him!

Just let him try and stop him.

Edmund paused a second, eyeing the doorknob of his hotel room door, and he took another moment, drew another breath, felt a fresh throb of the alcohol through his veins, and then he twisted the doorknob hard and thrust the door out into the corridor.

———

The hallway was empty.

Edmund stood there, in the middle of the darkness, and waited. His eyes shifted about the gloom, trying to find any form, to make sense of the shadows about him, to see just where the manager would be hiding.

He felt giddy, and a smile slipped onto his lips, and he was certain it was a maniacal one, splitting his cheeks in two. Because he knew that he was ahead, that he had done the right thing, that he certainly had the upper hand.

But he just needed that clue, that *first* clue.

A breath. A twitch. A *cough*.

Anything would do.

He stared out into the darkness, tried to harness every scrap of moonlight which sneaked in through the narrow, elongated window which stood at the end of the corridor, but no matter how hard he strained he could see nothing.

Nothing at all.

He took a tentative step, and then another. After the next it became simple. His heart thudded deeply in his ears, as if thrusting him forwards, pushing him on. And that slightly maniacal grin seemed to split his cheeks all the more, and his feet seemed to take on a mind of their own.

He was skipping now—actually *skipping!*—as he danced his way over the top of the stairs. He lingered there a moment, certain someone might be behind him, ready to push him down, but there was no one there. No one there at all. Perhaps it had all been his imagination, those sounds he'd heard of someone prowling their way up the staircase.

Yes, that was the explanation. That was surely it.

His wheelie suitcase *bump-bumped* its way down each step behind him, and Edmund made sure to keep his pace even, not wanting his suitcase to suddenly gain too much momentum and fly out from his grasp.

No, that would be a foolish thing!

As he came down to the final turn of the spiral staircase, he brought the lobby into view, and its ever-descending gloom. The lights were off. He slowed his pace, growing uneasy again.

But, why? He had heard the manager going upstairs, he *knew* that he was up there on the fifth floor now. There was simply nothing he could do to stop him now. Let him skulk about up there, on the upper floor of the hotel. Let him do whatever it was he was thinking to do!

. . . Because Edmund was leaving scot-free and, what was more, he wasn't going to pay for the whisky he'd drunk. From the state of the service in the place, he knew that he *deserved* a free drink for having given *them* the pleasure of his stay there.

The wheels of his suitcase knocked hard against the wooden

floorboards of the lobby, and they rolled hard against the surface as he made for the front door of the hotel. As he drew closer to the door, and he could feel his warm breath against that ever-colder draught blowing about the lobby, the thought that this was just too easy struck him.

But he scratched it from his mind.

What was he thinking? That this was some sort of a challenge cooked up for him to do? This wasn't some team building session: not paintball or some other bollocks.

No, this was just a spooky old hotel tacked onto a backwater town.

And he was getting shot of it.

He reached for the door handle, his fingers clutched a hold of the brass knob and, again, he was surprised at the quality, at the craftsmanship of the thing. Whoever was responsible for the Hilberthrudge Royale's descent into disrepair, and lunatics, ought to have been thoroughly ashamed of themselves.

He turned the knob, felt the sturdy mechanism give way, and then he gave the weighty door a good shove. It opened before him, showing off the car park out there, and a little snow sprinkling down outside.

The wind blew chillier now, and he felt the frosty bite to it. Perhaps his car would take a little encouragement to start, but no matter. He would get there, get inside, and if that massive bastard decided to set foot outside of the hotel front doors, Edmund would unclasp the glove compartment and slip out the pepper spray he kept there.

If that didn't do the trick, he'd snatch out the Taser too.

One or the other would take the big man down.

He stepped out onto the bristled-up welcome mat, so scuffed up from all the thousands—tens of thousands?—who had stomped on into the Hilberthrudge Royale when it had been in its own golden age, however long ago that was.

And right then, reaching into the pocket of his jacket for the car key fob, he heard a voice, whiny and familiar and, in obvious discomfort, coming from behind him.

". . . Father?"

Edmund turned back to look into the lobby, his heart welled in his throat.

8

EDMUND'S EYES played tricks on him all over again. Those shadows, the gloom, it just refused to take on any solid form, and he felt that chill of the wind creeping up his spine. The voice, of course, had been his son, Henry's, voice. But the illogicality of it, of the whole thing, only served to confuse him further, not to strike him with terror.

What was Henry doing here?

Why would he be here?

Could *this* be a trick?

Edmund opted to leave his suitcase where it was, on the doormat, and then he glanced back at his car, thinking of that pepper spray, of the Taser snug in the glove compartment. He could fetch them and re-enter, go investigate all over again.

Or should he just run?

Why shouldn't he just get the hell away from here?

From his previous encounter with the manager, he had every reason to expect an oddball trick like this . . . though it did raise other questions, namely: how would the manager, first, be able to imitate a voice so perfectly, and, second, how would he know to imitate the voice of Edmund's son?

We do not open the Hilberthrudge Royale in low-season for just anyone.

Those had been the words of the manager. But what had they meant? They were surely just the words of some madman . . . some madman or someone looking to confuse or irritate an outsider, someone from the outside world to these people.

Looking at it from their point of view, Edmund supposed they saw him as a kind of invader, and he was certain that they didn't want him here among them. Bumpkins were *always* like this. Of the ones he'd met, in any case.

And yet, he simply could not shift from his spot, lest he miss another rendition of the voice.

Only when he clenched his right fist did he remember that he had the car key fob there, when his skin came into contact with the smooth plastic, and the cold key itself. His fingers felt unwieldy, almost too unwieldy to squeeze the button.

But he managed it.

Off over on the other side of the car park, his car gave a little *beep* of its horn and flashed its hazard lights a couple of times. The dim interior light also blinked on, shedding a halo-like glow all around the car.

Forgetting his suitcase on the doormat, Edmund rushed across the car park, slipping several times on the iced-over surface, but catching his balance before he took a tumble. That would be just what they'd like, him to slip and break a bone. That would make things perfect for them. Then he would *never* be able to get away.

He reached his car and snapped open the door on the driver's side. He leaned over, undid the lock on the glove compartment. He slipped both the Taser and the pepper spray out from their little, velvety, drawstring pouches.

He had bought those pouches so that he could keep those self-defence weapons inconspicuous, so that, to his mind, if some overly nosey mechanic, or car cleaner, decided to go prying through his glove compartment—and he *knew* they could spring the lock if they really wanted to—then they wouldn't have the great joy of reporting the matter to their no-doubt policeman brother or sister, or cousin, or uncle, or whatever.

That was the thing with *plebs*, they were always looking for a way to get their own back from their betters.

Well, right now, Edmund had no need for those pouches, and so he discarded them in the floor space of the passenger's seat, and then ventured back across the car park, and back towards the hotel.

When he reached the door, he already had the Taser on, what the salesperson had described to him as being the 'Standby' mode, and he held his finger on the button, ready to let fly with those electric hooks into the manager's lunky mass.

The salesman had also assured him that the shock would be sufficient to bring a cow to its knees.

In his other hand, he carried the pepper spray, his finger hovering over the button, ready to deal any damage he thought necessary.

Edmund slunk back in through the doors, his head swivelling all about, keen to chase away any mysteries that lurked in the shadows. He gripped both his weapons tight, and knew that only death would be sufficient to get them out of his crooked fingers.

As the dim moonlight made some inroads on the almost unsurpassable gloom of the lobby, Edmund strode onwards, the floorboards creaking beneath his feet, and that *damn* draught growing a tad chillier still.

Was it just him, just the adrenalin and anticipation ripping through his blood, or was it colder in *here*, than it had been outside, in the car park?

He stared to the armchairs that stood with their backs to him, facing the extinguished fireplace, and to that cornice—the *cornice* the manager had spoken to him about. The cornice where *he* had heard the voices.

And then he looked to the fireplace. Was there someone there? Inside of it?

He stalked closer but still couldn't be sure. As he glanced round, to the windows of the lobby, he saw that the sun was just sneaking its way up on the trees, beginning to lay its gentle rays onto the tops of the leaves. But the lobby still remained steeped in the shadows. In darkness.

Over his head, he heard water pumping through a pipe. And he caught a whiff of that dankness that ripped through the air, and he felt his heart tap-tapping at his tonsils. The dry taste of whisky lolled on his tongue and he wished, more than anything else, for a drink of water.

He stepped onwards, drawing closer all the time to the fireplace, and to the form he was certain that rested there.

The rising sun flushed a slight pink glow through the windows of the lobby, and for the first time since he'd arrived, Edmund could get a proper look at his surroundings. At the lobby about him. In *day*light.

He turned slowly round, to face the fireplace, now able to get a proper look at it in the fledgling sunlight.

And there, sitting bound to a wooden chair, was his son.

Henry.

9

THE DRAUGHT got so cold in the lobby that it sent a chill shuddering right through Edmund, and his heart skipping about all over the place. He almost let slip both the Taser and pepper spray from his fingers, but he clung on at the last, his thoughts refreshing his mind, reminding him of the impending threat that lurked all about him.

That *he* had to keep himself aware of the danger.

He stole closer, his lips moving now, but no sound coming out. He took in Henry's face, his frightened eyes in the pinkish glow from the sunrise, and he saw that his son was crying.

Hard and profusely.

And he wanted to calm him. He wanted to put his arms around him and tell him that everything was okay. But, first, Edmund needed to know just *why*, just *what* had happened here. How was this, any of this, even possible?

He drew level with the pair of high-backed armchairs which stood opposite the fireplace, and then he stopped, his eyes lolling onto his son. And, finally, he managed to find the words. "What . . . what are you doing here? What have they *done* to you?"

Henry's eyes rolled upwards in their sockets and then rolled down again. Only now did Edmund see the bruises collected about his son's temples, the bruises about his eyes too. They served as a kind of eye makeup, like they'd just been painted on there for a theatrical performance.

No, looking closer, in the brighter light from the sunrise, Edmund could see that they weren't bruises at all. No, he could even tell from the smell of it.

It was ash. Soot. And as his eyes flickered over the chair, he saw that a pair of ropes were tied on tight to the back of it, and he knew that the voices from the cornice, the voice that he had heard, had been from his son, tied up there, hidden just a little way up the chimney.

Earlier there had been a fire burning there. It was a miracle he was still alive.

"Son?" Edmund said, his voice wavering in his throat. "Speak to me."

Henry met his eye and, his lips quivering, said, "Father, you . . . you *came* for me."

Edmund hesitated, unsure about how to answer the question. And then, as if something dawned over him, a pragmatic process bled into his thoughts. "Why aren't you on holiday? I thought you were in the Caribbean. What are you *doing* here?"

A slight smile curled the corners of Henry's mouth, and a slight twinkle passed over those glossed-over eyes of his, a small flush of pink from the sunrise peering in through the windows. "I . . . I saw the account, the account nearby here, the one you had on your desk, and I thought that I could come out here, that I could come to close it for you." His Adam's apple bobbed in his throat. "I thought it might give you confidence, enough confidence, to give me a promotion in the company."

"You lied? About going on holiday . . . so you could come here? *Impress* me?"

Henry nodded slowly.

Edmund wasn't sure what to think about the whole thing, and, as he admitted to himself, the most important part of all this was to get his son free. They could talk details later on. But right now their priority had to be getting *the hell* out of this place, and getting as far away as they could.

Despite the adrenalin roaring through Edmund's veins, and his brain screaming at his body to run away, he felt a twinge of pride at the back of his mind, and he knew that it was because he was, deep down, proud of his son. That he'd taken the initiative. All right, so he'd managed to get himself into a spot of bother in this *bizarre* hotel, but, then again, hadn't *he* done just the same? Fallen into the *same* trap?

He stalked forwards and almost immediately caught the flash that passed over Henry's eyes, and he stopped just where he was. "What?" he said. "What is it?"

But before Henry had the need to reply, Edmund glanced to his sides, looked into those high-backed armchairs, and he saw that each of them . . . one sitting in each . . . was the lobby boy and the hotel manager.

Each held a rifle in his hands, and pointed it at him.

Their eyes were dead, and their complexions like dried leather, as Edmund took them in with the light from the sunrise dribbling in through the lobby windows.

And the blackness at the end of each barrel of each rifle was complete and disorientating.

The manager spoke. "Put those weapons down."

———

For a couple of moments, Edmund was struck with shock. He couldn't believe it, that they'd been sat here, that he'd walked right into this trap. That Henry hadn't warned him.

He glanced back over his son's face, trying to find some note of deception there, but his son was only staring into his lap, his shoulders shuddering as he drew breath. And Edmund knew that his son was stuck in a daze, no doubt suffering from smoke inhalation . . . why, if he'd truly been up there in the chimney all along then he'd had no end of opportunities to call out to him, and hadn't. Only now had he pieced together some semblance of lucidity.

"I will not ask again," the manager said, his voice solemn, deep, elemental.

Edmund did as the manager asked, and he listened as the

pepper spray and Taser clattered down at his feet. He waited a couple of heartbeats and then, still looking to his son, but addressing the manager, he said, "What do you want?"

Henry's head continued to loll about on his shoulders as he remained fixed in his daze, lost to it.

Edmund had had enough experience of executive, high-powered politics, to know blackmail when he saw it.

Though Edmund didn't dare meet the manager's eye, he could tell, when the manager spoke, that there was a smile in his voice now. "We're looking for investment," the manager said. "Looking for some money to *invest* in the Hilberthrudge Royale."

"How much?" Edmund said, keeping his voice level, somehow finding the timbre that had served him so well in countless business transactions, the one that had earned Eastern Investments so many multi-million-pound deals.

Now he needed that voice to earn him back his son.

"Mm," the manager said, "a few million ought to do it."

Edmund sunk his teeth into his lower lip, because he knew that he would have to pull a bunch of strings to get his hands on that sort of money. But he would do it, if that was what it took. He had very little choice.

Didn't he?

"Fine," Edmund said.

"Shake on it?"

Edmund felt a lump form in his throat, and he couldn't take his eyes off his son, as if looking away for so much as a fraction of a second might mean that he'd disappear, or that they'd whisk him off up into the chimney again, keep him prisoner there.

Edmund stuck out his hand, and then looked into those chocolate-brown eyes once again as he shook firmly on the deal. Then he nodded to his son, tied up to the chair. "Good, now let him go."

The manager gave a dry chuckle. "No, Mr Stanforth, I'm afraid that simply won't be possible. Not at all."

"Why not?"

"Your son is our leverage, our way of getting just what we need. And we can't simply allow him to go away, without getting our own part of the bargain."

Edmund felt the sweat leaking down his face, dripping down to the collar of his shirt,, and then tickling its way over his pectoral muscles. "What, then? What do you propose?"

"We propose that you can go, that you can go to bring us the *money*. When you return, then we shall consider your son's fate."

"Fine," Edmund said, knowing that there could be no other way.

"Don't try to contact the police or anyone else, for that matter. You must remember that this is a small town. Everything that goes on, any *impending* raids, or whatever, they shall all pass to our friends in the Sesney Police Station." He paused a moment and, though Edmund couldn't bear to look at him, he was almost certain he was licking his lips. "And even if they don't, even if some *private* detective shows up on our doorsteps, and tries to break the deal, then I cannot guarantee your son's survival."

Edmund swallowed hard, and then said, again, "That's fine. Just fine. Now let me go, won't you?"

"Just one more thing Mr Stanforth."

"Yes?"

"One more thing that you should be aware of, of what we're capable of."

"Go on."

"When you've brought us the money, and we've set your son free, then you must forget all about us, you must forget all about the Hilberthrudge Royale. Just pretend it never happened. Scratch it from your past."

Edmund had no other intention.

"Because, if you don't, you must realise that we can use the same forces that brought your son here, that brought *you* here, to bring another that you care for."

A dozen swearwords flashed across Edmund's mind, but he somehow kept a stopper on them all, not letting so much as one pass his lips. He thought of those others. Of his wife, of his *daughter*. Or perhaps they could somehow get hold of his sister, or brother. There was no telling.

But what was he thinking? Was he just going to believe what this one nutcase said? Sure, the Hilberthrudge Royale was a great big, heaving pile of damp and rotting wood, but that didn't mean it was, what . . . *haunted?*

Why, that was just about the most ridiculous thing he'd ever heard.

Just then, the draught grew stronger all of a sudden, and it chilled him right to the very centre of his heart. And he thought about how he'd ended up here. *He* had made the decision to come here, he had been sure of it. It had been *his* choice to come all the way out here and close his account . . . well, his personal assistant had dropped the case on his desk, and he'd taken it up.

Another chilly rush passed through him.

Was the manager saying that he had some sort of *influence* over Edmund's personal assistant too?

This was just all so ridiculous that it didn't even bear thinking about.

All Edmund wanted was to free his son, so what was the point fighting it?

Edmund forced himself to look round, for him to meet the manager's chocolate-brown eyes once more, and this time he felt this inexplicable *thing* pass between them. What was it? Kind of like a *crackle* of electricity, was that it? Yes, something like that.

For some reason, he looked to his feet, to the Taser resting there, as if that might've been the cause of the sensation, but he knew, deep in his gut, that same gut that had got him so far in business, flagged him up to a bad deal, or something *odd* about a prospective client who—more often than not—had turned out to be one worth avoiding.

He trusted his gut, and what his gut told him now.

And his gut told him there was to be no funny business.

That he was to do just what this man said.

No more questions or deliberations.

Of that much he was sure.

"You may go now, Mr Stanforth. We shall be waiting."

Edmund thought of saying something, of saying something at least to his son. But it was all he could do, took all the energy he sucked up inside himself, to look over to where his son sat, on that chair—*roped* to that chair—and to give him the merest shred of a smile.

Because he knew, right here, in the Hilberthrudge Royale, there was forces at play far, far beyond his control, forces that he knew were far from his ability to combat. He was simply a pawn in whatever game he'd found himself in the middle of, and he had to act as such.

And so, with his head bowed, he turned away from the fireplace, and trudged back off across the floor of the lobby, the sun now risen over the tops of the trees, and setting the whole room in a flurry of diamond-like light. It would've been a beautiful sight if his gut hadn't been wrenching itself rotten, and his brain hadn't been feeling like a sodden sponge.

And if his son hadn't been held hostage.

———

Edmund sat behind the wheel of his car for the longest time. His eyelids drooped down, and he heard his heart thudding along hard. In the near distance he could hear birds twittering in the trees, and that fresh smell of dew-soaked grass seemed to ebb its way into his car. He sucked on his teeth until he felt a flash of pain through his gums, and then he turned the ignition.

He felt the steady *throb* of the car engine passing through the steering wheel, and through his fingers, where it seemed to judder at his bones. And he felt his mind unfurling itself, coming unstuck once more.

And, just as he released the handbrake, and took a final glance back at the Hilberthrudge Royale, he breathed in deep and screamed long and hard till the very base of his lungs ached, and he could feel shards of pain burrowing themselves deep into his brain.

He only thought to stop when he reached the base of the hill, and he was back on his way through the tight, tidy, quiet rural roads, and heading back through Sesney, going along the route that would lead him back to the motorway, back to the city, away from all this craziness.

But not for long.

INVISIBLE TO THE NIGHT

T HE AIR WAS MOIST TONIGHT. Devlin could smell rain coming. He drew his anorak tighter about himself, breathed in its tangy, sweaty smell. His *own* smell all mixed up with the waterproof material. He could hear the gentle, sticky slick of the soles of his shoes as they met—and then broke away from—the soggy pavement below his feet.

If there was one thing that he knew for certain—knew to be his creed—it was that while slitting throats in the darkness it was an impossibility to ever be caught.

Oh, of course, he realised that, in theory he *could* be caught, but, really it wasn't an option which he would spend any time considering.

Because then he would be trapped.

Trapped.

And nobody would ever *trap* him.

Not again.

He had made that promise to himself long ago.

Devlin held the knife down at his side. He had swiped the knife from his landlady's kitchen drawer. She would never suspect a thing. Not from the preppy, good student, what with his v-neck sweatshirts, and his dislike for wine, women and song. Even if she noticed the knife missing, she would not *ever* suspect that it had been *him* who had taken it.

He had selected this particular knife because of its recently sharpened edge.

He was very pleased indeed to have a nice *sharp* edge to work with.

That was the thing with slitting throats—it could be clean, it could be easy, but only with the right tools . . . otherwise you were liable to make a *nasty* mess.

No, all things considered, he was happy with his knife.

Now all he needed was a target.

As he strode down a side alley, which ran alongside the main road of the town, he caught glimpses of Friday night. Of the flimsily clad women: in their short skirts, their arms folded across their chests as if this might offer them warmth.

Another killer might've found fixation here.

But not Devlin.

He lived his life to avoid cliché.

And he was determined that he would be remembered for his originality.

Not for his brute strength.

What he was looking for—what he was *determined* to look for —were others.

Others like *himself*.

And so those on the bustling Friday-night street, the muscled men with the long-sleeved white shirts—*always rolled back to the elbows*—did not interest him. It wasn't that their shaved heads, or their mean expressions, caused any sort of fear to rise within.

No, that wasn't it at all.

He did not believe in acting out of fear.

That was how a person went and made mistakes.

He strode onward, through the side alleys, always keeping to the shadows, and—above all else—keeping the knife out of sight.

When he reached the end of the next street, his eyes lingered over a likely target.

He held himself still, forced himself to stop breathing.

He thought about how he had once gone hunting deer with his father, back when he'd been a teenager, before he'd started at university. They hadn't been hunting in such a long time now.

Not since his parents had got their *divorce*.

And his mother had taken the estate; had banished his father to his city flat.

Had banished his father from his rightful countryside.

Perhaps Devlin would never go hunting with his father again.

But he would never give up hunting alone.

Devlin took in the boy before him: glasses, a broken nose, and a gawky, skinny frame. Yes, this was promising. Very promising. If only he could see a little more—could see that the boy was truly alone. That there was nobody lurking in the shadows nearby.

Nobody to shout out, or to warn him.

. . . If he had been going on his gut instinct, he may well have lurched out right away; have gone to slitting the boy's throat.

But his logical mind kicked in.

Told him to bide his time.

And so he did.

He held himself still.

Waited for his moment.

And then he *struck*.

MIRACLES

1

PAULINE COULD FEEL THE ULCER, up high in the inside of her left cheek. She tried not to think about it. She attempted not to prod it with her tongue. Or to glance it with her teeth.

Because either of these actions sent pain shuddering through her.

And a taste of blood swirling through the base of her mouth.

The long leather jacket which she wore, which had once belonged to her grandfather, smelled strongly of marijuana smoke. A couple of weeks ago, she had leant the jacket to her nephew for a costume party, or some other hijinks, and he had returned it to her in this condition. With this *smell*. And, to top it off, with a missing button too.

Pauline supposed it had been a *good* night.

In the distance, she could hear the *whisper* of traffic from the motorway. Although this compact town seemed to be almost in the middle of nowhere, that sound was some sort of proof civilisation never dwelled too far away. That *reason* wasn't completely alienated even here; the most remote of spots.

As Pauline walked about the periphery of the premises, she had to admit that she didn't see all that much amiss. She peered in through the chain-link fence, eyed the curled-up barbed wire which was attached to the top, and the only real observation she came away with was that outside visitors were not wanted *inside*.

Not without pacing through that security lodge by the front gates, in any case.

To be fair, though, that was in keeping with any old warehouse, or factory, or any other sort of commercialised private land.

What, she supposed, made this a special case had to do with

the fact that this particular location sold itself as nothing less than *miraculous* ground.

Here, what she had been called into investigate, was the prevalence of such miracles. Of a man, on the other side of this chain-linked fence, within those many stainless steel-shelled, sludge-green buildings, who *claimed* that he could do everything from curing the common cold to making people walk again.

If it sounded sceptical to her mind then that was the least of it.

All her life, whenever people would pay her to do so—and *often* when they did not—Pauline would check into these potential fraudsters.

Do her level best to expose them for the snake-oil salesmen they surely were.

Because, even if they deluded themselves into believing that they had some sort of special power, that was just what they were.

Once she had completed her sweep of the premises, she returned to her eighteen-year-old estate car. It was gunmetal grey and had a dent present in just about every square metre of its bodywork. All the rubber trimmings had come away from years of abuse: from Pauline subjecting it to snow, to ice, to dust. And, for whatever reason it was, the maintenance of her car always seemed to fall down near the bottom of her list.

Her maintenance of *anything* seemed to fall down near the bottom of her list.

Sometimes she wondered if the reason she hadn't had a steady relationship for about the duration she'd had the car was because of her lack of tidiness.

She would meet women. She would call them once or twice. She had her devices—ways to bring them close. And then she used similar tricks to send them away again.

Into the arms of others.

Or simply away from her . . . for their own protection.

Feeling a slight chill entering the air, she stuffed her hands into her jean pockets. Some dead leaves skittered past along the ground. A few caught themselves on her body, and she brushed them away, feeling that rough, bark-like texture to them.

Winter was, well and truly, here now.

It'd be Christmas before too soon.

And it was sure shaping up to be a lonely one.

With a sniff, she snapped her mind back to the present moment.

She glanced up again.

There was something *off* about this place, that was for certain.

This compound seemed to carry a note of conspiracy to it.

There were two possibilities at stake here:

One, that the subject of her investigation was just who he said he was. That he really *did* have powers to cure the ill, to heal the sick. And he had become so successful, so well-known for doing so, that he had to take extreme measures.

He had to hide himself away here, in these buildings.

In the middle of nowhere.

Just so his business wouldn't become overwhelmed.

Or, two, it could be that the subject's operation *was* a complete scam.

And that he kept himself here in the hope of steering clear of discovery.

By necessity, she had to believe the second eventuality.

Her client, in this case, was a journalist. One of those rich kids who'd found themselves promoted for a position that they never really wanted. *Paying* somebody else to do the snooping for them.

Oh, he had claimed that he had legitimate reasons—that he had already written a few pieces on the subject, and he would be recognised by the stringent security checks. The fact that Pauline, as a notorious private investigator of all things fishy might have better luck in terms of navigating the background checks seemed to slip past her client.

But she wasn't complaining. Neither was she *consciously* judging anybody's character. Anybody who paid her bills was all right with her.

As she stood by the side of her car, staring down on the compound, she wondered just how she was going to get inside. The place seemed to have tighter security than some prisons.

2

PAULINE'S CLIENT, it turned out, was not entirely useless. He hadn't *just* left her there with nothing at all—to go about the case as best she could with no resources. No, as he had assigned her the job, he had handed her over a folder containing all sorts of goodies. Among these was an appointment sheet: a printed-off confirmation for precisely ONE MIRACLE.

It really *was* in block capitals.

She couldn't help her eyes slipping down the printed page, and to the text at the base which, in polite legal terms, declared that there would be no refunds.

When she caught sight of the price, saw that it ran into four figures, she thought she could see why. The overhead of this place had to be ludicrous.

A series of signposts indicated the entrance to the compound. 'Security' was euphemistically termed 'Bookings Office', and Pauline brought her car up to the window of the booth, and let her engine idle.

Up ahead, she took in the red-and-yellow barrier which blocked her path. It was just like those devices that were placed at the entrances and exits to car parks. She also noted the security camera which hung down from just above.

Moments later, the booth window slid back, and Pauline found herself staring a gruff-looking, bald-headed man in the eye. He wore a suit and, unsmilingly, he asked for her confirmation form.

When she handed it over to him, she noted how he attempted to look past her, into the car, no doubt searching for anybody that she was trying to sneak in for a bit of *extra* healing.

The man filed the confirmation form off to one side, unseen behind his window. When he glanced up again, she saw he had a dark-green chit clutched in his hand. It had the number seven printed on it.

She waited for him to hand it over.

But he held back.

He fixed her with his blank stare. "What was it that you've come to see Edwin about today?"

Pauline fluttered her eyelashes. Though she was under no illusions about her appearance—she used *no* makeup after all, and she had her hair cut short in a way which didn't seem to appeal to men—she hoped she might communicate a sort of ditziness.

Just as she imagined most of Edwin's customers were ever so slightly ditzy.

The guard continued to eye her closely.

"A pain in my right hip," she said.

The guard held her gaze. He tilted his head to one side.

She thought she saw something snap in his eye.

Some decision being made on the spot.

And, for the longest second, she was certain he was going to lift the barrier, give her instructions on where to park.

But he didn't.

He got up, rolled his shoulders and said, "Mind if I take a look at your car?"

Pauline felt her chest tighten.

When the security guard emerged from his booth, he was much squatter and bulkier than she had imagined. He rounded her car twice, before pushing his face right up close to the glass, using his hands to shield his reflection as he peered in. He wore a grey-blue jacket over a pair of slightly tatty black combat trousers. He had tucked the legs of his trousers into the tops of his ankle-high boots.

Finally, the guard ended up around the back of the car. He nodded at the registration plate.

"Don't match the record," he said.

Pauline silently cursed her client.

"Nothing major," he said, "just one of the digits ain't right."

Pauline sensed the guard's slightly bored tone, and she realised that he was just following procedure, that, most likely, he didn't have much of a suspicion *specifically* about her.

"Got any ID?"

" 'ID' ?" Pauline found herself repeating, again trying to sound a touch ditzy.

Perhaps a little drugged up to help with the pain.

She dug around in the inside pocket of her jacket, aware that she was probably wafting that stench of marijuana over the guard as she did so. Then again, didn't people use marijuana for pain relief? Finally, she produced her ID.

Well, it wasn't exactly *her* who was named on the ID.

Rather, it was one of her many fakes.

She had to take care in using her real name when she was on cases, she knew that these various frauds were all notoriously careful about their background checks. Her *false* name would've already surely run the gauntlet and been given initial approval.

The guard handed her back her ID. "All right, Mrs Wilson, you can go through." He sniffed a couple of times, apparently close to catching the same cold that Pauline could feel coming on. "Do you need any assistance at all? Any help with mobility?"

It was then that Pauline realised she had made her first mistake.

And there was little to no point in pretending that she hadn't now.

She had got out of the car *all* too easily.

Without enough of a show of strain.

But she brushed it off.

She had to.

She was a professional.

"No, thank you," she said, with a light smile. "I should be fine for a couple more hours yet."

The guard nodded and—just like that—gave the security camera above a casual wave.

Pauline had been checked out.

And found to be *clean*.

The security guard had *assumed* that she was medicated up to her eyeballs.

3

A S THE GUARD DIRECTED, she drove around the back of Building C. She parked up her car in the spot marked 'Visitors'.

That done, she got out of her car and trod up to the tinted-windows of the double-doored entrance. There was a keypad there, and the red light glowered at her.

She supposed this was where she was meant to wait.

This place was more like a sports centre than a 'Miracle Factory', as the newspapers had often dubbed it. How her *client* had dubbed it.

She thought about the news report she had seen a few months ago. As she'd driven in along the rural roads, she had seen the scarred, torn-up earth at the sides of the road where the transmission vehicles had parked while their reporters scoured for interviews.

That had been the day after a man had been wheeled into the 'Miracle Factory' before walking his way out.

Even when she had seen the news report on TV, while crunching her way through cereal, she had thought it too good to be true. And she thought it too good to be true now.

The 'cured' man, for one.

The very *fact* that his first reaction, once he had been given back the ability to use his legs, had been to go public sat uneasily.

Because she knew that wherever money and miracles were concerned there was almost certainly a mystery to be unravelled.

The magnetic locks buzzed open.

And the doors opened automatically on their well-oiled hinges.

There, standing in the opening, she saw the familiar grinning face of Edwin.

As in all the pictures in all the papers, he dressed smartly, in a waistcoat, a clean white shirt on underneath. Pauline could also see the gold watch chain which hung from one of the pockets of his waistcoat, and she supposed that was, no doubt, an acquisition from the money he had plundered from the helpless, and the hapless.

He welcomed her in, with a sweep of his arm, and she examined his well-trimmed grey beard which matched his grey hair. His eyes were a light blue even though Pauline had always thought that they were a dark brown. It was one thing to see a face in a photograph, and quite another to see it in real life.

As Edwin guided Pauline through the corridor, she took in the high roof above their heads—it stretched up at least six, or seven, storeys. She could make out the corrugated steel pattern above. And the metal ribs which helped support the weight.

While they walked, slowly at first, and then getting ever-increasingly faster, as if Edwin was testing out Pauline's affliction, he explained his personal history with his premises.

"Wouldn't work anywhere else, *see?* What I require here is space—space for my tools—and peace and quiet." He came to a halt, reached out and took hold of her forearm in a gentle but insistent grip. "That's the most important thing, don't you think? *Peace and quiet?* For what else could a person ever want, for what other reason are you here, aside from wanting a little peace and quiet?"

She really couldn't think of anything to respond with, so she simply nodded and gave him a slight smile. To show him that she *was* the bimbo he thought she was.

Finally, after staring longingly into her eyes, as if he was searching for something located within her irises—and, as far as Pauline knew, he was—he released her and they proceeded on their way.

Continuing along the corridor.

They'd been walking for what must've been about ten minutes, along those labyrinthine corridors, before Edwin brought them to a halt outside a door. This door, like the exterior one, had a keypad for typing in a letter-and-digit password.

Edwin quickly tapped in a code, turning the light from red to green.

His tapping was so practised—*so swift*—that she really never had a hope in hell of getting to catch more than one or two of the numbers or letters.

Not that, really, she needed to know.

Because it would be quite an operation to try and breach the chain-link fence outside.

They emerged into a corridor which had beige carpeted walls. Several fake plants. No windows. The air smelled of rubber, and Pauline—*annoyingly*—brushed that ulcer of hers once more with the outside of one of her molars. She grimaced.

Edwin halted.

He turned.

His eyes searched Pauline's face. "You are in pain —aren't you?"

Although Pauline was fairly confident that that much was apparent by now, she had to admit that there was something odd about him picking that *exact* moment to turn around and ask her about it.

And, though the pain was somewhere else than where she had described for the guard, Edwin reached up with his hand and she felt his soft well-moisturised skin brush her cheek.

At first nothing happened.

And then there was an—*almost unbearable*—warmth.

It pulsated through Edwin's fingers.

And into her skin.

She felt every hair on her body stick up. A tingle ran down her spine. Her heart dipped in her ribcage, so far that she was vaguely afraid that it might end up in her stomach.

The taste of blood in her mouth was now almost too much for her to bear.

She had an overwhelming urge to swallow.

But could not.

It was like . . . with his touch . . . with *Edwin's* touch . . . she was rendered paralysed.

He held his fingers to her cheek. A slight smile curled his lips and he tilted his head to one side as if he was trying to see her from a different angle. Trying very hard to understand her at a profound level.

"You came here to expose me, didn't you?" he said, his voice still full of warmth—*good* humour.

She wanted to clench her fists. She wanted to beat him away. But she knew, at the same time, that there would be no hope of that. Not now.

Somehow . . . *somehow* . . . he held her trapped.

He had done something—*Not magic! Not magic! Not magic!*—but he had caused some change to happen in her. Some drug?

. . . If it had been a drug then how had it been administered?

Because she could recall neither drinking or eating anything that she had been offered. And the guard had never come close enough to jab her with anything . . . unless . . . her mind switched back, in a haze, to their face-to-face chat when she had first come in . . . Edwin, he had . . . had gripped her forearm tightly . . . had he done something then, had he taken his opportunity then . . . but even so . . . how hadn't . . . hadn't she . . . noticed?

It was then she realised she could no longer control her eyelids.

They simply drooped down.

As if her own body was putting her to sleep, saying:
Lights out! Sleep tight!
And though she fought it, in the end, she had to give in.

4

WHEN PAULINE CAME TO, the darkness almost overwhelmed her.

She had only that thick scent of rubber.

And a taste of copper . . . no, *blood* in her mouth.

Her stomach felt like it was twisted into knots.

Footsteps sounded all around her.

Whispering voices.

She reached out. She could feel a mattress beneath her. It was springy. She could feel herself sinking down into it. When she attempted to sit upright, her head began to spin. She had difficulty remembering where she was.

For some reason, she believed she had been in a car accident, that she had—*somehow*—driven recklessly and got herself into trouble.

Gradually, a dim light came into being within Pauline's room.

She could make out the shapes—the *shadows*—at first.

Still those footsteps.

Still those whispering voices.

The light got brighter.

Soon became *too* bright.

It took all the coordination that she could muster to bring her arm up to shield her eyes from the glare. Finally she gave up and shut her eyes all over again.

In some far recess of her mind, she heard a door creaking open.

Heard a familiar voice.

"Pauline . . . Paul . . . Paul . . . *leen*?"

She brought her arm down from her eyes.

Looked to the doorway.

Saw the silhouetted figure there.

A man in a white lab coat.

A *doctor's* coat?

As her eyes slowly made sense of the finer features, she saw that he wore that same silky waistcoat, the crisp clean white shirt beneath that.

The grey hair.

The well-trimmed beard.

And the gentle loving smile.

Edwin.

Again she attempted to sit herself up in bed, but she had no success.

Her muscles would not remain straight.

"Please, Pauline, just relax—that's the only way you'll have peace and quiet."

She felt as if her brain was rapidly expanding and contracting, pushing against the constrictive prison which was her skull.

"Would you like to know how it's done, Pauline? Isn't that why you came here? Isn't that why people like you *exist?*"

She couldn't bear his tone of voice.

Edwin's voice.

It curdled her blood.

Sent a fizzling sensation up to her brain.

If only she could get herself up.

If only she could *stand up*.

She could handle herself just fine.

She could fight him off if she had to.

If he *made* her.

With a dizzy scrabble, she attempted to grab hold of one of the metal railings of her bed. But, even when she made contact, she couldn't form a fist. No sort of grip at all.

That didn't stop her trying, though.

She tried and tried and tried . . . then tried some more.

But she could get no purchase.

"Pauline, are you going to sit still and listen to me?"

She felt the world humming around her now. The bloody taste in her mouth was replaced by the flavour—or at least the *texture*—of rubber. Just that nothingness inhabiting her mouth. Taking it over. Smothering out any form or detail or recollection.

She could already feel her eyelids drooping again.

She knew it wouldn't be long before she had to let go.

Before her conscious mind would have to let go again.

And she would be lost—*once more*—to drug-addled sleep.

"The 'Miracle Factory', " Edwin said, and even though Pauline couldn't clearly make out his face, she knew that he was smiling warmly. "A funny name, and perhaps a little more accurate than was intended, because, and listen to me carefully, please, Pauline, everything here is about giving people peace and quiet—what they so *desire*."

She could hardly stitch so much as a strand of memory together. It just seemed like everything was getting away from her. That even the reason . . . the *reason* . . . she was here . . . it seemed to . . . to escape her.

"It's really quite simple," Edwin said, with no small amount of pride present in his voice. "People pay us *money*—just as you did, under that pseudonym of yours—and then we bring them in here, and we *cure* them of whatever it is that ails them." He paused for a long moment. "Doesn't that sound pleasant?"

Pauline peered at the silhouette of Edwin.

She wished she could see his face clearly.

Wished she could peer into his eyes.

Because then—*then*—maybe he wouldn't sound so smug.

Then she would . . . would be able to . . .

"Now, please, Pauline," Edwin said, "if you wouldn't mind just relaxing a little, or I'll need to call an orderly in here, hmm?"

She hadn't been fully aware that she *was* fighting.

But she let the tension leave her muscles.

And it seemed to do the trick.

Edwin continued, "Those who come here to be cured, their hope, well, I'm sure you agree, it's awfully inspiring. Very noble. The challenges these people go through in their lives. And they come here, hoping for me . . . for my *magic* to set them right again . . . make them *walk* again . . . have them cured of some *incurable* disease."

She felt a touch more lucid now. She could recall why she was here.

That she had come here.

That she had wanted to *expose* Edwin's operation.

That he was—*right now*—telling her all his secrets.

If only she had an audio recorder, or a notepad, anything . . . anything but her tired, addled brain!

"Well, Pauline, for you it shall come as no surprise to learn that there *are* no miracles—that those who cannot be cured *cannot* be cured." He paused. "And that's where the other branch of our operation comes in—where those who need a new life, for whatever reasons, we are not picky as long as they can provide the money, come to us."

She gazed over herself, to the shape of her body outlined by the sheet draped over her. She could get away from here. She could escape. If only she could grab control of herself again . . . if only she could make herself *walk* again.

"And we give them a new life—the lives of those who *enter* here, to be precise. We take the faces, the builds, and we place them onto those who enter through our back door. The ones who walk out of here—why, they're changed, forever, of course they are. And it is so funny that I have never heard a relative complain about personality changes; they're just so glad to have their loved one back at full-operative capacity."

Pauline's mind dug up, from somewhere, that little note she

had read on Edwin's website, about how the treatments here would take up to three months.

And that those wishing to be cured would be kept here all the while.

This . . . this was the reason why!

She felt that she had strength now, strength enough to speak words. To make the effort with her tongue, and to put them to Edwin.

"Wha . . .what . . . happens . . . ?"

But her strength failed her now.

Edwin struck up a new smile. "Don't worry, Pauline, we'll take good care of you here, but I'm afraid that you won't be allowed to leave"—here his smile widened—"which is to say that *you* won't be allowed to leave in *that* body of yours. But another, not unlike you, and certainly bearing all the familiar features of Pauline *shall* leave here.

"It really was a masterstroke of yours to come walking in with that pseudonym—I shall leave it to the new Pauline to decide on whether to slip back into *your* life or to carve out a new life of her own, as Mrs Wilson."

Pauline could feel her heart thumping hard now, and that was despite whatever drugs Edwin had administered her in an attempt to keep her calm, and under control.

She had to escape.

Needed to escape.

Edwin remained standing in the doorway. "Don't worry about being lonely Pauline. Look around you."

For the first time since she had woken—since her every waking thought *hadn't* been preoccupied with Edwin standing over her—she looked about her.

Saw that there were other beds.

Other people beneath the sheets.

Those who sought *cures*.

Edwin glanced at his wristwatch, then said, "I suppose that I should be going now, I have matters to attend to." When he looked up at her, he was grinning. "Another few miracle seekers. Others seeking peace and quiet, well, I can honestly assure them that they'll find it here."

Pauline looked to the other beds scattered around her, to the apparently lifeless figures inhabiting them. And she knew that she would become just another.

"Merry Christmas, Pauline," Edwin said.

He turned out the light as he left the room, shutting the door behind him.

THE STONEMAN

1

ROAD FLIES BENEATH HIS LORRY. Getting all swept up. The white lines are hypnotising. Almost like stars soaring past the port window of a space shuttle. The air is stale. Emptied packages fill the floor space of the vacated passenger seat.

Stoneman grips the wheel. He tastes blood in his mouth. A broken tooth in there too, perhaps. He can hear the *rumble* of the lorry engine and he imagines his vehicle a mother bear—and him her cub. He can feel it soothing him. Massaging his weathered flesh. And his rattled-about bones.

A long, straight stretch opens up before him.

Nothing but that blue-grey of road.

The sprouting greenery on all sides.

Cars buzzing about him like fat, lazy horseflies.

The motorcycles like mosquitos.

Stoneman peels his strained fingers off the wheel. He cracks his knuckles.

One.

Two.

Three.

Four.

The thumb makes five.

He eyes his mirrors. Does the full sweep. Flips the indicator stick. Listens to the percussive *tick-tick-tick-tick*. The blinking orange light catches the corner of his eye. He drags the wheel to the left. Makes for the slipway leading off the motorway.

And up, up, up . . . away from the rushing madness.

The bland nothingness of the road.

Just for a while.

Stoneman circles the roundabouts with expert precision.

Though he has never been to this specific place before, all these roadside services have a pattern to them. Patterns which are scarred upon his subconscious mind. He picks out the restaurant: a chain diner by the name of *Toby's Tucker*, and he pulls into the car park awaiting him there.

Stoneman steps down from the cab of the lorry. He pulls the visor of his baseball cap down to cover his eyes from the sharp sunlight. His aviator sunglasses keep most of the brightness away. He rolls his long-sleeved, denim shirt up to his elbows. He drags the waistline of his jeans up his gut. He kicks his boots—one after the other—against the steps to the lorry cab. Not because he has mud clumped onto them, but because it's a force of habit. He grew up on a farm. And whenever coming in, or going out, he would have to kick something on or off.

His eyes don't so much as look as absorb. But where the information goes, Stoneman really has no idea. It's as if the images which open out before him simply soak through his brain, like water through a sponge.

He can't control it any longer.

Control vanished a long time ago.

He takes in the parked-up lorries there. Half a dozen of them, at least. And he chews over the couple of drivers standing about at their cabs chattering away.

Stoneman, though, has no time for chatter.

He has a Purpose.

A Purpose much greater than himself.

He leaves his lorry behind—his safe space—and he treads over the well-worn tarmac to the entrance of the eating establishment.

Toby's Tucker, he thinks to himself, *Sounds friendly*.

Inside of *Toby's Tucker*, the air smells of disinfectant, and blood, but that might just be Stoneman's faulty nasal apparatus. He always smells blood. Everywhere he goes. When he breathes in the disinfectant it causes his mouth to dry up, his tongue to feel a little like a soaked cotton pad left out in the sun too long so it's got all crispy and matted. He can hear some music playing over blown-out speakers. The song plays too quietly to be identified, but he can track the unmistakable rock-and-roll beat. He longs to be back in his lorry.

But not yet.

Almost.

But not yet.

Stoneman observes the décor of the diner. A fifties-styled place. Those booths up against the windows with the cushioned benches on either side. Perhaps it sparks a recollection inside of his mind. Or maybe it's just Noise. Most things are just Noise so why should this be any different?

He sees an empty booth.

He takes a seat there.

When the waitress comes by to take his order, he sees that she is in her late forties—or maybe her early fifties—and that her blond hair, once golden, now bears strands of silver. Her lipstick is smudged. Her eye shadow looks more a black eye than makeup.

He orders by pointing out what he wants from the menu.

He says nothing to her.

Not through his lips.

When she takes his menu off him, she mutters something under her breath that might or might not be a swearword—some sort of an insult. But Stoneman pays it no mind.

He has a Purpose, after all.

And everything else is just Noise.

2

WHEN STONEMAN FINISHES UP HIS BREAKFAST: scrambled eggs on toast with a cup of black coffee, he sets his mind to his Purpose once again. Thinks about just what he must do now. He has learned to follow his instinct—his instinct hasn't steered him wrong yet. Sometimes it comes quickly, other times it's a matter of patience.

Whichever one happens, he knows that his Purpose shall make all clear.

It doesn't take long till Stoneman feels the old familiar twitch.

That little sense telling him that . . . *now* . . . *now it's time!* and he finds his attention drawn in by the boy standing over at the till of the diner.

The boy must be eighteen or nineteen. Maybe even older than that. Stoneman has never been a good judge of age. His Purpose does not encompass such superficial judgement calls. The boy has fair hair which hangs down to the cusp of his neck. He carries a backpack which seems too bulky for his skinny frame. As he stands at the counter, paying for his meal, he clutches the straps of his backpack as if eager to shove off.

Stoneman sees the cardboard sign beneath the boy's arm.

The one which reads 'Dorthmarch.'

His destination.

Just where Stoneman happens to be going himself.

Stoneman hoiks himself up off the comfortable cushioned seat of the booth. He trudges towards the boy. The boy, Stoneman can tell, is already tracking his approach out of the corner of his eye. The attendant at the till hands the boy his change and the boy gets all fidgety. He attempts to stuff the cash and coins into his pocket.

But in his hurry some of it drops.

Coins tinkle about his feet.

One of them rolls right into the toe of Stoneman's boot. Stoneman crouches down to fetch the coin. He clasps it tight between his index finger and his thumb. He inspects the golden coin in the sunlight which tumbles in through the windows of the diner. For a few seconds, Stoneman's focus on the coin blurs everything else out. And then he sees the boy. Standing there. Staring at him. Just beyond the rim of the coin.

Stoneman smiles.

He shows his well-brushed teeth.

Appearances are important.

Even somebody with a Purpose like Stoneman can see that.

The boy smiles back.

Nervously.

The boy holds his hand out for the coin.

Stoneman holds back a playful second. He lays the coin down in the boy's palm.

The boy closes his hand around it.

Stoneman pushes the visor of his cap up a touch. He eyes the boy's sign. "Dorthmarch, huh?" he says. "That where you're going?"

The boy blinks several times. Taken off guard. He glances down at his sign as if only now realising that it was there at all. He looks back at Stoneman. He nods his head. "Uh huh," he says.

"You got a ride?" Stoneman says.

The boy seems torn.

Stoneman can tell that the boy smells it.

That he smells the blood.

That he *knows* danger lurks here.

But, perhaps due to naivety, maybe because he simply cannot think, the boy says, "Not yet, no."

Stoneman gives the boy a nod. He jerks a thumb back over his shoulder. "I can take you as far as there," he says.

The boy's eyes widen. Maybe out of surprise. Perhaps out of fear. But then he says, "You don't have any problems with company policy? I mean, I asked around here, asked a few of the drivers, and they said that they can't take hitchhikers."

Stoneman remains silent.

He knows that completing his Purpose relies—more than anything—on subtlety.

He can't push the deal.

That might bring everything crashing down.

Stoneman eyes the boy through his sunglasses. "I work alone."

The boy remains torn. He seems on the cusp of smiling, only the smile can't manage to break its way out onto his lips. He glances back at the attendant at the till as if she might be able to shine some light on this thing. But, already, she's sorting the notes and coins into their trays. Too busy to preoccupy herself with the outside world.

And who can blame her?

Stoneman continues to smile at the boy and then he says, "So, you coming, or not?"

3

OUTSIDE, in the car park, some of the lorry drivers are putting their heads down for a nap. Stoneman sees them drawing the curtains. He can hear the music coming out of their cabs, or the sound from the films playing on concealed screens within.

It's not night yet, but, at the same time, night's not a long way off.

The boy stands and stares at the side of the lorry. Worry lines appear in his brow. He looks at the dirty white tarpaulin which covers the side of the lorry. He glances back at Stoneman. "Why don't you have a company name on the side?"

Stoneman holds still. He knows that he can't push this. Anything like this.

He needs to be patient.

"Like I said," Stoneman replies, "I work for myself."

The boy, though, remains unconvinced. He glances over his shoulder. Perhaps hopes to catch somebody's eye. But to what end, Stoneman is unsure. Does the boy wish to cry out for help? But where's the danger? What *evidence* does he have? Isn't Stoneman doing him a favour by carting him along, taking him on his way?

The boy seems to shake off his doubts. He looks to Stoneman. He gives the trace of a smile. He walks towards the cab.

Stoneman lets himself into his side of the cab. He clambers up to the driver's seat while the boy—like some ethereal mirror image—does the same. Stoneman fixes his hands to the wheel. His fingers pressing into the familiar ruts in the plastic covering, he knows that what he does is right.

That his Purpose, and nothing else, serves him now.

When Stoneman starts up the engine to his lorry the mood

inside the cab is utterly changed. Now when the gentle thunder passes through his fingertips, Stoneman feels excitement. It seems that his lorry has shifted away from being the mother bear keeping watch over her cub to being a snarling grizzly, just baying to take a bite . . . if only the prey would allow it.

Is Stoneman the real monster, or is it the lorry?

Who is to say?

Stoneman pulls out of his spot. The *beep, beep, beep* of the reversing notification sounds. Stoneman keeps his eyes fixed on the mirrors, but, at the same time, his thoughts are enclosed on the boy sitting on the seat beside him.

The boy now has his rucksack resting on his lap.

Stoneman smiles at him. "You can put that down at your feet if you like."

The boy seems uncertain for a couple of moments.

For a long second, Stoneman is certain that the boy will flee. That he will reach out and grab hold of the door handle. Throw himself out while he still can.

Before they hit the motorway.

But the boy stays still. He smiles back vaguely at Stoneman. He sets his rucksack down at his feet just like Stoneman asked.

Stoneman completes the manoeuvre. He pulls onto the slipway.

Heads down.

Onto the motorway.

THE CLOUDS ALL BUNDLE UP OVERHEAD. Their soggy bottoms threaten rain. Stoneman can *smell* the rain through the ventilators of the lorry. He can feel the chill of it up against his skin. He can *taste* the slightly salty flavour on his tongue. He listens to the gentle *rumble* of the tyres finding the road beneath him. The way that they simply soar along as if the surface was nothing but clouds and air.

A speck of rain splatters the windscreen.

Another.

And another.

Stoneman flips on the wipers. He watches the mechanical arm smear the water across the glass. And he thinks of blood. Of freshly spilled blood.

He almost allows the sensation to get the better of him, but the boy speaks.

He takes Stoneman's mind off it all.

"Up ahead," the boy says, pointing.

Stoneman sees the sign. A campsite. Four miles.

The boy turns in his seat, glances at Stoneman sidelong. "You can leave me there—night's coming. I should probably get some sleep and start out fresh tomorrow."

Stoneman remains silent. He knows that his Purpose will not allow for this. It will not allow for prey to slip loose from a trap. To do so would be against Will. It would be a betrayal of himself. And his lorry.

He resolves not to let go.

Never to let go.

"I drive through the night," Stoneman says.

The boy says nothing in reply.

Rain falls harder.

Minutes pass.

The boy remains silent.

Stoneman watches for the sign. For the turnoff to the campsite. He sees the boy looking. His neck craning to follow the road which snakes up and away from the motorway. On towards the field. Stoneman sees the many pitched tents.

An hour passes.

Neither of them speaks.

Stoneman realises that he is now reaching the moment of truth. That, now or never, he shall have to make his move. To do anything else would be against his Purpose.

He glances over his shoulder. "In the back," Stoneman says to the boy. "There's a bunk. You can sleep there if you like."

The boy says nothing. He continues to stare out through the windscreen.

The scenery whizzes past.

"We'll be there in a few hours," Stoneman says. "I'll wake you."

The boy stays where he is. Sitting on the seat. Staring.

Stoneman knows that he is thinking. That some basic survival mechanism within is warning him. Telling him to run. But the chance to run has disappeared. If only the boy had been more insistent back when they'd passed the campsite.

Maybe then . . . *maybe* . . .

The boy reaches out. He grabs hold of the steering wheel.

Stoneman sees him coming. Just fast enough. He keeps the lorry within its lane.

A car passes by.

Horn blaring.

Lights flashing in the dusk.

Stoneman looks to the boy. Sees him grabbing for the door handle. But there is no door handle there. Stoneman removed it long ago. The boy soon realises. He glances back at Stoneman, a new fear in his eyes. Soon, though, the boy's mind switches. He comes up with a new plan.

Stoneman slows the lorry, brings it onto the hard shoulder.

More blaring of horns behind.

But Stoneman pays them no mind.

He knows that he has his prey cornered.

That there will now be no escape.

The boy now hammers his fists against the window of his door. He tries to break through. And then what? Does he plan to run? To take off running through the long grasses? To lose himself in the forest beyond? Does he truly believe that Stoneman will cease to chase him . . . or does he only hope?

Stoneman brings the lorry to a halt. The hydraulics hiss out. The cab slumps a little.

The boy moves away from the window. He ducks down to his rucksack at his feet. He scrabbles through the compartments. He searches for something.

But Stoneman is ahead of him.

Stoneman reaches into the compartment below the steering wheel. He whips out a rope from within. Gnarled. Frayed. Blood-stained. The boy won't be the first victim, that's for sure. But surely the boy realises that now. The boy shall be in good company.

The boy tears open one of the zip-up pockets of his rucksack. He produces a Swiss Army knife. He flips the longest blade out from within. The blade sheens in the light from the cab. His skin seems almost the same shade as the grey, silvery knife. The boy holds the knife up to his nose. His hand shakes. The knife is undulled. Most likely unused. Stoneman knows that the boy is not accustomed to doing harm to others. And that will count against him.

If the boy ever had a chance before, that chance is fading.

Stoneman holds the rope clutched in his fists. He squeezes it.

Feels its rugged texture. This will all be over so soon. Sooner than the boy will be able to fathom. If only the boy would go quietly. It would be *so much* easier.

The boy backs up. Against his door.

Stoneman remains in his seat. The rope still in his hands. He knows that the only way for the boy to escape is for him to push past. And there's little hope of that. He selected the boy for his scrawniness. The boy wouldn't be able to knock Stoneman down in a million years.

Not even with that knife of his.

Killing does not come easy.

Even when it's your Purpose.

The boy glances about. Now it seems that even he has acknowledged that he will be unable to strike with that knife of his. He simply does not possess the detachment. That all-important ability to simply switch off from the world. To see things for what they really are.

To bring a living thing to its end.

Stoneman does, however, possess those abilities.

He could not be more dominant.

The boy draws a long breath. He screams out. So loud that it sends a shudder down Stoneman's spine. A chill through his blood. Stoneman grips his rope tighter still. Stoneman knows that the ending is coming. That the boy wishes to call for help that shall never arrive. The only sound outside of the lorry is the *whoosh* of the passing cars on the motorway. At best, even if the boy managed to break free of the lorry, he would only receive a whole host of horns.

Nobody would stop to help.

Nobody *ever* stops to help.

Stoneman knows that from experience.

The knife slips from the boy's grasp. It tumbles down into the floor space of the passenger seat. The boy doesn't scramble for the knife. He knows that it will serve him no good. His lips move soundlessly. His hands crumple up to his chest.

Almost like he's praying.

Stoneman holds the boy's gaze. He keeps his expression solid. Unmoving and unmoveable. He can feel the Purpose deep within himself. He knows that he will win out.

The boy speaks a single word under his breath. A *hopeless* word.

If only somebody would be here to help him.

If only the boy had turned Stoneman down in the diner.

This moment never would've rolled around.

But isn't this what they call fate?

Stoneman holds back a longer time. He stays focussed on the boy while he reaches up for the cord to the curtains. With a gentle *zip* of the cord, he listens to the mechanism shut the cab of the lorry out to the rest of the world.

Night-time inside.

And out.

5

STONEMAN DRIVES ON into the dawn. He watches the gentle pink light glowing up on the horizon. He loves to drive along at this time. Something about it seems entirely perfect to him. He only notices the flashing red-and-blue lights when he looks for the third time.

He expected this.

He knows that he did.

There was no other way.

Somebody—*sometime*—had to find him.

And now they've tracked him down.

He reads off the lettering on the bonnets of the three cars trailing him.

The only traffic on the road at this time.

Police.

Stoneman watches them catch up to his back fender. He sees the driver frantically gesturing for Stoneman to pull over into the hard shoulder. Stoneman obliges the driver. He brings his lorry to a halt at the side of the road.

He glances down to the floor space of the passenger seat, to the boy's rucksack which remains there. He can see the Swiss Army knife there too. The blade still flicked out. Ready for use by somebody with a firm, killing hand.

Somebody like Stoneman.

Stoneman remains in his seat as he observes the police leave their cars behind. They draw their guns as they round his lorry. As they come up, one on each side of the cab, another officer stands back a little further, covering his colleagues.

If only Stoneman could make them understand.

Understand that, now, he has completed his Purpose.

That this world requires nothing more of him.

Then they would see that they didn't need those guns of theirs.

That he is, quite simply, no threat to them.

But how might he communicate such a thought?

One of the officers opens the passenger side of the cab.

It's not locked from the outside.

Another opens the driver's door.

The officer who stares in at Stoneman looks angry. His face all wrinkled up in fury. "Get out! Get out *now!*" he says.

Stoneman, holding up his hands, does as the officer asks.

He steps down onto the virgin tarmac of the hard shoulder.

Another two officers are pointing their guns at him now.

Another is going through his cab.

Maybe they think he has a bomb inside there.

Something to blow them all away.

But, no, he has nothing like that.

The officers lead Stoneman around his lorry—around to the back.

"Open it up!" the first officer says.

Stoneman stares at the back of the lorry. At the door which winds up, and down, depending on how he wishes.

The officer jerks his gun at Stoneman's chest. "I said *do it!*"

Stoneman holds himself still. Slowly—*working so slowly*—he reaches for his pocket. He digs about there for the keys to the lorry. He selects the key from the ring. He slips it into the keyhole. He turns it. Already, without so much as thinking about it, he breathes in.

He breathes it all in.

He tugs on the metal cord beside the rollup door.

Listens to the mechanism catch.

Tug its way upwards.

Slowly. Slowly. An inch at a time.

He feels the police all watching now.

All their attention fixed on the space opening up before their eyes.

Will they imagine it?

Is this a surprise for them?

Or have they been briefed?

Has some earthly soul given Stoneman away?

Stoneman cracks open the door all the way. He shows them the insides. One of the policeman blinks on his torch. More torchlights follow. Behind him, Stoneman hears one of the officers vomit. Another does the same. He hears the *splash* of it on the tarmac.

And then—almost right away—Stoneman feels one of the officers tugging his hands behind his back. Cuffing him. That cold bite of steel.

Already Stoneman can feel himself floating away. As if being carried upwards by a cloud. All his work—his *Purpose*—all spread out in the back of the lorry.

Ready for them all to see.

On the way in the back of the car, Stoneman hears the officers speak about him.

Curse him.

But he knows, deep down, that what he did was right.

It was more than right.

It was what he was put here to do.

His *Purpose*.

FIND FIVE LIMBS

1

BABY SCREAMS PIERCED the flat's paper-thin walls. Eric juddered awake and bent his neck to glance at his clock. Seven thirty. Nothing like a sleep in. He rubbed his eyes, threw off his duvet and padded along the hall.

His son, Peter, stood up in his cot, gripping the bars. Eric cooed and Peter's wails turned into moans. Peter raised his arms into the air and Eric swept him up. For a moment the entire apartment submerged into silence. Eric took deep breaths and shut his eyes. It might be the only moment of peace he got in the whole day.

The phone chirped in the kitchen. Eric crooked Peter in one arm and jogged toward it. He arrived just as it rang off. "Bugger."

Peter pointed at the phone. "Dah."

"Yeah, how about that?"

"Dah."

Eric set Peter down and clicked on the coffee maker. It whirred and sucked on the grounded beans he'd lined it with the night before. His mind sprang into action and he looked at the kitchen clock. The babysitter was supposed to get to the flat at about seven, but she was always late, which in turn made Eric late for work. If only he could find a decent woman, someone willing to mould herself into his dated concept of gender roles. That would make things much simpler. Unfortunately Peter's mother hadn't wanted to fit that description.

Peter plodded about the kitchen, stumbling every couple of steps but always catching himself on a kitchen cabinet or somehow regaining a precarious balance. He reached up to the kitchen counter.

Eric's mind remained numb a second longer then he noticed

the meat cleaver perched on the kitchen counter. The early morning sun peeked through the blinds, sending a shimmer across its blade.

Eric's heart leapt into his throat and he stepped over to the cleaver, seizing it before Peter had a chance for another grab. The babysitter must've left it out the night before, nonetheless, he should've checked before going to bed. He knew there was no way a stranger would worry about his son to the extent he did.

Peter clucked to himself and seemed to forget all about the cleaver, instead focussing his attention on a shiny button lying on the kitchen floor.

Eric replaced the cleaver on the magnetic rack above the stove then bent down to retrieve the button. "Well, I suppose we'd better get you washed and dressed, don't you think?" The phone rang again. Eric snatched it up. "Yeah?"

"Collins?" It was Detective Gravesend. His partner.

"What's happened?"

"We've got something."

With the phone resting between ear and shoulder, Eric reached down for Peter, hoisted him up and cuddled him to his chest. "Go on."

"An arm's turned up in a park."

"Jesus."

Gravesend read off the park name and details. They agreed to meet in an hour. Gravesend paused to swallow whatever it was he was eating then said, "How're you doing for childcare?"

Eric drew Peter closer to his chest. "Oh, getting along."

"Good. Listen, get out here as soon as possible. There's some people in high places that've got their eyes fixed on how this one's going to turn out."

Eric's gut twinged. Just what he needed. More pressure. He reeled in his worry and made an effort to keep his voice calm. "All right, be there in a bit." He hung up.

Peter stared at his face, his deep blue eyes examining his. A sense of wonder overwhelmed Eric. Sometimes it was hard to believe he was a father, that he was responsible for more than himself.

Eric broke from his daze then slung Peter over his shoulder, sending his son into a fit of giggles and squirming. "It's top and tail time for you."

2

ONCE HE'D GOT Peter into his clothes, Eric set him down on the bed with a purple stuffed elephant. He creaked open the wardrobe doors and perused his suits, settling on the one with the least amount of visible stains.

At seven forty-five the babysitter still hadn't arrived. If she didn't come, he'd have to cart Peter off to work with him. Was it even legal to have a toddler riding shotgun on a murder investigation? It was that or call Lauren, but they hadn't spoken for weeks. It was his fault really. His mind had just fallen apart since his last case bombed. No, Bea-Bea, as his babysitter liked to be called, was his only hope.

Eric stepped into his trousers, threw his jacket about his shoulders and tightened the knot on his tie. After a quick glance in the mirror, he decided there was nothing for it. He whisked Peter up and headed for the door, managing to pour himself a cup of coffee as he went. He yanked the door open, bringing himself face to face with Bea, her arm outstretched to knock. She wore a blue t-shirt punctuated with ducks floating down with umbrellas clutched in their beaks. Her hair unravelled like wool, brushing her shoulders.

Eric's anger subsided and relief settled over him. "Thank God you're here." He passed Peter over.

She accepted him in her arms and a grin spread across over her lips. "Peter!"

Peter's mouth contorted then he sniffled. "Bea, no. No, Bea-Bea."

"It's okay," Eric said, one foot out the door. "You'll be fine with Bea." He checked his watch. Almost eight. He swooped in for a kiss. Peter grabbed a tuft of his hair and Eric had to jerk himself free from the grip. "See you tonight, okay?"

"No, Bea-Bea."

"What happened this morning?" Eric said to Bea.

"Leaves on the lines."

"I'm running late now," he said. "We agreed seven."

Bea pouted and cocked her head. "I'm not your alarm clock."

Heat rose in Eric's cheeks. He hovered. He'd love to fire her, right there and then. How dare she get shirty with him?

"You'd better hop off to work then."

Eric gritted his teeth. "Yeah." He glanced at Peter and smiled. "You be good for Auntie Bea, okay?"

Peter reached out, a tiny hand snapping open and shut. "Dah, Dah, Dah!"

"Let's get you some breakfast," Bea said, sauntering toward the kitchen. She swung the door shut, letting it slam in Eric's face. He needed to find a new babysitter and soon.

Eric bounded down the steps to the car park where his medium sized family car awaited him. It was shaped like a matchbox and turquoise, functional if not attractive. He leapt inside, tucking in the tail of his shirt as he went, then headed out into rush hour, trying to get his head right for the job at hand.

3

ERIC SPIED Detective Gravesend before parking up. It was impossible to miss him, leaning against the red railings, stuffing a bacon sandwich in his gob. A portion of his vest peeped through the buttons of his shirt. Gravesend was living proof that the force's bi-annual fitness tests weren't what they'd once been.

Eric whipped out his flashing light from inside the glove compartment and plonked it on the roof to protect his car against overeager traffic wardens.

Gravesend nodded to him and mumbled, "Morning," through his half-eaten sandwich.

"You all right?"

Gravesend shrugged and swallowed the remainder of the sandwich. "Piles giving me a bit of gyp, but apart from that not bad."

Eric attempted a glance around Gravesend's bulk, toward the crime scene, but failed. "How're they getting on?"

"Drawn a blank."

"It's an arm?"

"That's it. We think it's female."

"Anything that stands out about it?"

Gravesend chuckled and released the railing. "Only that it's bloody missing its body."

"Shall we?"

"Come on, then. This way."

About halfway across the park, Gravesend laid his hand on Eric's shoulder and looked him in the eye. Eric prepared himself for another of Gravesend's famous mentor moments. "Look here," Gravesend said. "We all know about your ability. The secret's out."

Eric glanced down at his shoes, wondering whether he

should've given them a quick polish the night before. These little talks always made him feel self-conscious.

Gravesend continued, "You've just got to move on. Forget the last case. Get yourself together, yeah?"

"Yeah."

Gravesend tapped his nose. "There's people watching this. Your ticket's up."

"You think so?"

"Don't think your scores went unnoticed. You marked yourself out on those tests. All you've got to do is show something in the field and you'll be moving up a grade, I know it."

"If you know so much, why haven't you gone upstairs yet?"

Gravesend smiled. "Guys like me ain't meant to move up." He tapped his temple and widened his eyes. "Haven't got the brains for it. In any case, if I got promoted they'd make me lose a shedload of stone. Nah, it's not for me."

Eric looked over at the crime scene. Indeed, a man in his mid-sixties, with thin-framed glasses, wandered about. He looked senior. Eric remembered seeing him in the canteen a few times. Perhaps Gravesend wasn't bullshitting for once.

Gravesend sighed. "All right, politics to one side, shall we get on with it?"

Eric followed Gravesend to the crime scene. Gravesend stepped over the yellow tape, puffing out his cheeks like he was nailing some assault course. Eric ducked under. A pair of forensics meandered about with test tubes clutched in their fists. Gravesend led Eric over to an area covered by a small off white canvas, a few square feet in size. Both men crouched down on their haunches and looked underneath.

A dismembered arm lay under the tarp. It had been cut just above the elbow joint and white bone stuck out at a blunt angle. Eric covered his mouth with his hand and repressed the grumbling in his stomach. "Looks like a hacksaw job."

"Yeah, should be open-and-shut this one. Once we get on the trail. Amateur's work this."

Still crouched, Eric crabbed his way around the arm. "Any distinguishing features?"

Gravesend reached out, groaning with the effort of suspending his chubby arm. He indicated a tattoo just above the wrist. "Just this."

Eric leant closer. A few blotches. "It's like the ones we used to do at school. You know, with ballpoint pens."

Gravesend straightened up and winced. "Bloody hell. What kind of school did you go to?"

Ignoring him, Eric said, "The ink's fresh."

"Killer did it, then?"

"Yup." Eric ran his finger across mid-air, a few inches from the tattoo and read it, "Fourteen, fifty-six. What is it? A date?"

"Maybe. We ran a search in the pool. Birthdays, years, months, those combinations, but nothing's turned up."

"Historical killers?"

Gravesend screwed up his eyes. "Think you've been watching too many films. Next thing you know we'll be off down the library, looking stuff up. "

Eric's phone buzzed. He slid it out from his pocket and pressed it to his ear. "Collins speaking."

"We've turned up another one."

"Go on."

"It's a leg. Same body."

Eric got the address then smiled at Gravesend. "Seems like we're heading to the library after all."

Gravesend blew out his cheeks. "My lucky day."

4

THEY TOOK ERIC'S CAR. Eric laid his mobile on the dashboard and shot off with the siren blaring and light blazing. While running a red light, Eric noticed his phone buzzing.

"Want me to get that?" Gravesend said, already reaching out. He placed it to his ear. "Hello? . . . Yeah, this is his phone . . . He's driving . . . Uh huh . . . Yeah . . . Fine . . . Okay . . . Yeah, I'll tell him . . . Yup . . . Bye." He sighed and replaced the mobile. They sat in silence a few seconds.

Eric shifted up to fourth and looked over at Gravesend. "Well, are you going to tell me who that was?"

"Your babysitter."

Lightning danced up Eric's spine. He clutched the wheel tighter. "And?"

"Asking if you want her to pick anything up for dinner. They're heading down to the shops."

Eric wrinkled his brow. "Typical. Whenever I ask for anything slightly outside the role of"—he released the wheel and made quotation marks with his fingers—"'nanny,' she always kicks up a fuss. Maybe she's cottoned on that she's getting the sack."

"Why's that?"

"Peter hates her."

Gravesend scoffed. "Bollocks. All my kids hated their nannies growing up. You're best not sacking them, mind. Better just to let them get bored and quit." He rubbed his thumb with his index finger. "Cheaper."

"Yeah, well, just hope she won't quit the day a body turns up."

Gravesend shrugged. "Someone like you must have some lateral thinking skills. I'm sure you don't need a thicko like me dishing out advice." He snorted up a wad of phlegm, wound down the window and spat. "Waste of my time and yours."

Eric scanned the road name and spun the wheel. Someone beeped behind him and tyres squealed.

Gravesend clutched the dashboard. "Bloody hell. Next time I'm driving."

Ignoring him, Eric checked out the building to his right. There was a large sign which read: Yewtown County Library. The council logo blazoned on the side. "Looks like this is the place," Eric said, bringing the car to a stop.

Gravesend scowled. "Fucking hate books."

"Why?"

Didn't start reading till I was nine, did I? More of a telly man. Books made me freeze up."

Eric slipped out of his seatbelt. "This is the perfect opportunity to make peace then."

"Smug bastard."

A pair of officers guarded the car park. Both looked solemn and stood silently. They had pale skin and wrinkle-free faces. Perhaps this was their first body. Eric marched past them to the cordoned off area where another small tarp was set up.

Gravesend drew up alongside Eric.

Eric inspected the leg. "It's got a tattoo, like the other one."

"Really?"

"Yeah, take a look."

Gravesend produced a packet of crisps from the pocket of his jacket. "Nah, you're all right." He ripped the packet open and shovelled a handful of crisps into his mouth. "Whatever happened to going postal then doing yourself in? That's what I want to know."

One of the officers tapped Gravesend on the shoulder. "Excuse me, you can't eat here. You'll contaminate the scene."

Gravesend took a step back, lunging his legs as far as they allowed. "How's that, poindexter?"

The officer sighed then returned to guard the tape.

Eric inspected the tattoo. "It's another number. Ninety-three, forty-six. That mean anything to you?"

"What do I look like? A fucking computer?"

Eric rose and dusted off his hands. "We'd better have a chat with the librarian. Might've seen something."

Gravesend crunched through his crisps. "Suit yourself. I'm just here to keep you on the straight and narrow. Stop you slapping people about."

"And I'm so very flattered."

"Don't mention it."

They trudged up to the library door. Its red paint peeled back to reveal a dull, blue-green undercoat. Eric rang the bell and took a step back. They waited half a minute then Eric rang once again.

"Playing with themselves in the back, no doubt," Gravesend said.

A bird-like woman poked her head around the door. Her eyes darted between the two officers. "I'm sorry. The library's shut today. You'll have to come back tomorrow. Talk to the officers outside, they'll tell you why." She made to close the door.

Eric jammed his foot in the crack. "We're police."

Her complexion paled and she swallowed. "Oh. You've come about the leg?"

"We just want a moment of your time."

She seemed to float backward. Eric and Gravesend stepped inside.

A smell of sawdust and cheap perfume pervaded the room. Eric restrained a sneeze. The librarian waved at a pair of blue plastic child-sized chairs. "Take a seat, please."

Eric sat and turned to observe Gravesend. It seemed a physical impossibility that it would take his weight. Nonetheless, Gravesend sat down, using his arms to support himself on the table. He'd turned quite pale. Perhaps he really did have a book trauma.

"Were you the one who discovered it?" Eric said to the librarian.

"Yes."

"Did you see anything unusual?"

She shrunk into her chair and flashed her eyebrows. "Well, it's not every day a leg turns up in the car park, I'll tell you that for nothing."

Gravesend wheezed.

"Yes, I realise that," Eric said. "But anything strange about the scene, anyone hanging about?" Eric said.

"No," she said.

Eric arched his back. "We turned up an arm this morning. We think they're part of the same body."

"How horrid."

"Yes." Eric clutched his hands together and considered his line of questioning. "There are tattoos on each limb. A pair of double digit numbers."

"And, what about them?"

"Just wanted to know if there's anything familiar about ninety-three and forty-six?"

"They were on the leg?"

"Yes."

She squinted then pursed her lips, causing her mouth to resemble a beak. She looked from Gravesend to Eric. "No. Nothing."

Gravesend muttered something under his breath then got up. Eric hushed him back down. The chair groaned under Gravesend's weight. Eric said, "Think carefully about those numbers. There might be some connection. Something that will help us catch whoever's doing this."

"Ninety-three? Forty-six?" she said.

"Yes."

Her cheeks flushed. She considered for a moment then stuck a finger in the air. "Hang on a sec." She skittered across the room and slid open a drawer full of index cards. Her nimble fingers flipped through and she flicked out a card. "Those numbers are familiar."

Gravesend nodded at her hand. "That's it, is it?"

"Oh, no. This is just a reference card. To find the maps."

"Maps?" Eric said.

She got up from her seat and ran a well-practised index finger along the shelves. "I knew there was something about it. Yes. Yes, I remember now." She stopped and slipped a large book off the bottom shelf.

"That looks serious," Gravesend said.

She brought it over to the table and laid it down. It was about three feet across and covered in dust. She blew across it. Gravesend and Eric coughed, but the librarian didn't bat an eyelid. She swished through the pages, stopping occasionally to scan. Finally she stopped and tapped her finger twice. "This is it."

Eric came around and stood at her shoulder. The map was organised into a grid of tiny squares.

"Well?" she said.

"What does it mean?"

"This was one of the proposals for the organisation of maps. From the eighties. Each pair of numbers gives a location." She ran her finger along the top and settled on ninety-three. Then, with the other, she skimmed the side and got down to forty-six. Finally, she brought her fingers together. "And here we are. The library's in this square."

Gravesend blew a long stream of hot air from his nostrils and got up. "I'll be waiting in the car if you need anything. Sick of this brainy shit." The door slammed shut behind him.

Eric straightened up. "Can I borrow the maps?"

She examined the air above his head. "We're not supposed to loan out unless you're a member."

"I can speak to your boss if it's a problem."

Her eyelashes fluttered and she batted a hand. "Oh, don't be silly. I'm in charge here."

"So I can take it?"

"As long as you bring it back."

He snapped it shut, tucked it under his arm and headed out.

"Detective?"

"Yes?"

"Try not to get blood on it."

He smiled and pushed his way out. "I'll do my best."

The door swooped shut and he trotted up to his car. Gravesend sat in the passenger seat tucking into a jam donut. Where the hell did he get all his food from? Eric stepped in through the driver's door.

Gravesend produced a bottle of fizzy drink. He swashed it about his mouth, swallowed then nodded at the book. "What've you brought that for?"

"Might help."

"Does it tell you where the next one is?"

"No."

"Then what's the bloody use of it?"

"We know his system now. It's better than nothing."

Gravesend took another swig of fizzy.

Eric's phone buzzed its way across the dashboard. He caught it before it dropped off into Gravesend's sticky lap. 'Bea Calling,' read the screen. Not again. He squeezed his eyes shut then answered. "Hello?"

"Mr Collins?"

"What's the matter?"

"You didn't call back about the supermarket."

Eric laid his free hand on the steering wheel and gazed out into the deserted road ahead of him. "I'm a little busy."

"You could've called."

"Right. Can we talk about this later?"

She sighed. There was a clatter in the background.

His heart skipped a beat. "What was that?"

A pause. "Oh, nothing."

"You'd better see to it."

She hung up.

Gravesend burped. "What was that dizzy bitch on about this time?"

"Supermarket again."

"Does she always call this much?"

Eric sighed. "Yeah."

"Bit intense"—he winked—"good girlfriend material in that case."

Eric sat back in his seat and knocked his head against the headrest. "God forbid."

Once more, his phone buzzed. A message from headquarters. They'd found another limb. Eric shunted the book onto Gravesend's lap, no doubt smushing it in donut debris.

ERIC SCREECHED to a halt outside Kingsborough College. A group of kids dressed in grey uniforms buzzed about the entrance. Bass lines bounced from a pair of portable speakers which sat on the wall beside them. Eric wound up his window and stepped out onto the pavement. Gravesend rolled out of the passenger seat. He knocked back the rest of his drink, eyeing the building. Another burp then, "Bit of a shit heap."

"Yeah, well, it doesn't help when people like you don't pay your taxes."

"Pay what I have to and not a penny more." Gravesend let his bottle drop then kicked it into the gutter. It bounced a few times. One of the kids stared at Gravesend and the bottle, as if unable to believe he'd just seen a grownup do such a thing.

"And that's setting a great example," Eric said.

"What? They're not my kids. Shows them who's boss. Look at him." Gravesend pointed up the steps at the kid watching them. The kid promptly turned back around. "That's one more kid that'll think twice before nicking my dust caps."

Eric shook his head and climbed the steps. "You and Gandhi against the world."

The group of kids disintegrated around Eric, letting him through the reception to where a uniformed officer waited. Eric approached him. "How long you been here?"

"About half an hour."

"Where is it?"

"Toilets. Kid found it."

"Is the kid okay?"

The officer sighed. "Yeah, they're keeping him away from the other kids. He didn't get a chance to tell anyone else about it."

Eric spotted the sign for the toilets. "That's good."

"Wait here, shall I?" the officer said.

"Yeah."

Eric marched down the corridor, keeping his eyes fixed on the approaching toilets. Yellow tape surrounded the scene and another officer stood outside. He tipped his hat to Eric and held up the tape to allow him to pass underneath.

Inside the toilets it stank of stale urine and farts. Eric remembered flushing Year Seven heads down toilets. The corner of his mouth tweaked into a smile and he pushed back the cubicle door.

A leg was jammed into the bowl, its grey toes sticking out. Gravesend arrived, huffing and panting. He sidled up behind Eric. "Looks fake to me. Kids these days drop prosthetic limbs like sweet wrappers."

Eric remained focussed on the leg. Something about the sleek skin was familiar. Déjà vu? He shook off the feeling, read off the tattoo and noted down the number. "Check that will you?"

Gravesend juggled the map and flipped through the pages. His forehead crinkled as he ran his finger along the page to match up the reference. "Yup. This is the place." He handed back the notepad. "We done?"

Eric wanted a bit of space, to think without Gravesend breathing down his neck. "Give me a sec. I want to take a look about."

"I'm going to find a caff. Don't want to hang about too long in a place like this. Might turn me common."

Gravesend careened out of the toilets.

Eric walked back and forth, taking a glance into the cubicle and at the leg sticking up. He still had no clue who the murderer was or where he might strike next. Worse than that, he didn't even have an identification on the victim. He'd have to let forensics have a go. There was nothing here for him.

He inspected the sinks and stared at himself in the mirror. How had the killer got inside? Did they have something to do

A V IAIN

with the school? It didn't really matter. However it had happened, they had got in and done it. Pretty soon there'd be body parts all over the city, unless Eric did something to stop it. His temples throbbed with the weight of expectation and responsibility. If he didn't crack this case, he might as well say goodbye to any hope of promotion. He slammed his fist against the wall, bringing flakes of paint showering down. It was no use mooching about in a boys' toilet.

He slipped out his mobile and dialled up Gravesend. The call clicked through and there was a fumbling sound. The line went dead. He called up again. This time Gravesend answered. "Meet me at the car," Gravesend said, his voice quivering slightly.

"Why? Have they turned up another limb?"

Gravesend murmured something then hung up.

Eric's heart raced and he hurried out of the toilet, past the officer. Kids' faces filled the windows in the classroom doors. Although they didn't know what was happening, they'd seen the uniformed police. Why did these killers always get kids involved? Probably abused in their youth or something.

Gravesend stood propped up against the car.

"What is it?" Eric said.

Gravesend flipped out his phone and scrolled through the screen. He held up his call register for Eric to see. He'd highlighted Eric's name and number, the two calls he'd placed just now.

"What?"

Gravesend tapped his temple. "The tattoos on the limbs make up your mobile number."

Eric reached out and took the phone. "You're joking." He inspected it, matched it up to the numbers written on his notepad then handed it back over. "What does this mean?"

"He's playing games with you."

"But why?"

"Maybe you pissed him off or something."

"What about the other numbers?"

Gravesend shrugged. "Symmetry?"

"He just added another couple of numbers on a lark?"

"Could be."

Eric gritted his teeth, looked back at the school then stared at his palms.

Gravesend clapped him on the shoulder. "Come on. There's not much we can do about it for the moment. Just have to watch and wait."

6

WITH NOWHERE ELSE TO GO, they sat in the car and waited for the phone to ring. Around one o'clock, kids streamed out of the school, wandering toward the chippie at the end of the street. A couple of the braver ones cupped their hands and looked in through the tinted windows. Gravesend bashed his fist against the glass and they scattered.

Eric let the problem float about his brain. The first ten digits were his phone number, while the next two hovered in space. Another eight figures, two more body parts to complete the phone number. Find five limbs. After that, would there be more?

He shuddered. Maybe the killer would start on internal organs. How many parts did the human body have? They might need a microscope, the way things were going.

Up ahead, a white van jerked from the traffic and pulled to a stop. Its side door squealed open. A reporter emerged with one hand on a microphone and the other holding down her miniskirt. A cameraman, then a soundman, followed.

Gravesend brushed the crumbs from his suit. "Let's get away from here."

Eric checked his mirrors then ploughed out into the road. He trod the accelerator to the floor before the reporter had a chance to fire off a question. They rounded the corner and Gravesend pointed to the dashboard. The phone was vibrating again. Eric shifted gear then reached for the phone. "Hello?"

"Mr Collins?" Bea again.

Eric squeezed the phone between his ear and shoulder, taking the wheel in both hands. "What is it this time?"

She wheezed then coughed.

"Hello?"

"When are you coming home?"

"Why? What's happened?"

Another pause.

"Bea? Bea? What's the matter?"

The phone went dead with a click. A lorry pulled out and Eric swerved, almost clipping the front bumper. "Shit."

Gravesend clutched the sides of his seat. His cheeks looked gaunt. "What's got into you?"

Eric chucked his phone at him. "Take this, will you?" He gripped the wheel tighter.

"Who was it?"

"Babysitter again. She couldn't speak freely. Sounded like someone was there with her. I reckon it's the killer."

"Shit. Want me to call backup?"

Eric jerked the wheel and shot into the slow lane. He caned the car up the exit ramp and onto a roundabout where he flew off along the familiar route toward his flat.

They pulled into the underground car park. Orange lights flickered on, setting the place in a twilight gloom. Whoever this idiot was Eric wanted to take him on, alone. No one threatened his son, his family, and got away with it. He parked up and jumped out. "You stay here."

Gravesend opened his door. "You can't go up alone."

Eric unholstered his pistol and pointed it at Gravesend. "Get back in the car."

Gravesend held up his hands and got in. "Calm down. Let me call backup."

"Shut the door."

Gravesend slammed the door, sending the car rocking on its suspension.

Eric's heart pounded in his ears. He trotted up the stairs, both hands clutching the pistol, keeping it pointed to the ground. When he reached his floor, he pressed his back against the wall. Hands shaking, he reached out and shoved the front door. It wasn't locked. The door rattled on its hinges, rebounding off the interior wall. Silence. He wiped his palms on his trousers and adjusted his grip on the gun.

After a quick glance up the corridor, he strafed to the right. The kitchen was empty. Eric picked out the cabinet under the sink. It was a few inches open. He approached it and pulled the door back, praying it wasn't Peter.

A dismembered arm sat in a pool of browny-red blood. The bottles of cleaning liquid had been moved aside to give it space. On autopilot, Eric read off the numbers of the tattoo. He padded his pocket for his mobile then realised he'd left it with Gravesend. He squeezed the pistol tighter.

There was a note pinned to the fridge, across the room. It transfixed him. He stepped closer, hardly able to believe his eyes. Bea's number. The first two numbers matched the extra two numbers on the third limb and the middle part matched the four on the fourth. Fuck. But where were the final four digits? Where was the fifth limb?

Something twitched at the back of the flat. Eric released the safety and steadied himself. He inched his way down the corridor, toward his bedroom.

Inside, Bea stood with her back to the window with Peter held tight to her chest and the cleaver clutched in her hand. There was a smile sketched on her lips. "I didn't think you were coming, Mr Collins."

Peter's eyes were bright and beady, his cheeks puffy. "Dah!"

Eric lowered his gun. "Put the knife down."

"Where's the fifth limb?"

"I'm not saying. Not until I get assurances."

"What?"

"I want you to notice me."

"What're you talking about?"

"I go about trying to impress you, and you just ignore me like I'm a piece of filth."

Eric's mind stalled. She was delusional. Then, it all came back to him. Weeks ago, after the last case, he'd come home and they'd drunk a glass of wine together. Had she somehow interpreted that as a come on? It was hard to believe. Then again, he'd seen weirder things in this city.

Her lip wobbled. "You treat me like this."

Eric stepped closer. "Let the boy go, Bea. He's scared."

"I don't want to be lonely." She shifted her weight and brought the cleaver closer to Peter's skin. "Don't come any closer."

"Okay, sorry."

A tear ran down Peter's cheek.

Heat rose in Eric's face. He fingered the trigger. "Let him go, now!"

Bea swivelled around to hold Peter up to her face. "If you kill me, you kill both of us."

Eric attempted a smile. "Where's the fifth limb?"

"Getting ahead of yourself, aren't you? What about the first four? Did you find out who they were from?"

"No."

"Shame. I might've called those limbs in, one-by-one, but I don't like to just hand out answers. Makes people lazy. Won't you have a guess?"

"No."

"Oh, well. Spoken to Lauren recently?"

His pulse quickened.

Bea raised an eyebrow. "And it didn't click for you?"

Eric's blood boiled. He tried to keep himself steady and play to her delusion, wait for his opportunity. "Maybe we could be something, who knows?"

There was a series of thuds at the door. A backup squad.

Bea's eyes widened.

"I'll call them off," Eric said. "Give them some excuse. We can be happy."

She lowered Peter for a second and met Eric's eye. "Really?"

Eric aimed at her head and squeezed the trigger. The pistol clapped. A hole opened in Bea's forehead. Blood trickled down her face. Peter dropped to the floor. She slumped backward into the wardrobe.

Tension evaporated from Eric's muscles. He lurched forward and snatched up Peter, not pausing to take a second look at the babysitter's corpse. Together, they sat in the corridor and waited. "It's okay, now. It's okay."

Peter's tiny chest rose and fell in fits and bursts.

A few moments later backup burst through the door, knocking it from its hinges. Armoured officers marched past Eric and Peter, huddled on the floor. One of them peered into the bedroom. "In here, boss."

Someone shouted, "Clear!" and Gravesend waddled into the flat. He approached Eric. "You took her down?"

"Yeah."

Eric snorted back his tears. "Got an ID on the body."

"And?"

"Lauren Tinsfield."

"You knew her?"

"Went out a couple of times. Nothing serious," he said, feeling himself well up despite his stoic delivery.

Gravesend nodded then placed hands on hips and glanced into the bedroom. He returned with a whistle. "Cost a packet to get that cleaned up."

"Maybe."

"What you need is a nice little wifey. No more 'help wanted' ads for you."

"Tell me about it."

Gravesend exhaled then went off to talk with the leader of the backup squad.

Eric noticed a red mark on Peter's wrist. It ran with ink. A tattoo, just like the others. He reached out and touched it. Peter flinched. "Does it hurt?" Eric said.

Peter nodded.

"We'll take care of it." Eric cuddled him tight then whispered, "I love you," in his ear.

TENNIS FOR TWO

1

THE CROWD'S SCREAMS in his ears, Harold Frankly smashed an enormous forehand and gritted his teeth. It sliced through the air and whipped the line, sending up chalk in a triumphant puff. He pumped his fist and glared at Evan Guerrero, his opponent.

In the tiebreak of the final set, the scoreboard ticked over to 6-4 in Harold's favour.

One point from victory.

Up high, in the executive box, sat Trevor Purvis, the millionaire who'd promised the victor of the three-match series five million dollars. His gold chains sparkled in the late-afternoon sun.

Guerrero led the series 1-0. Harold had to win this match to be in with a chance of winning the prize money. And, God, how he needed it.

Harold sank into his chair and wiped the perspiration from his forehead. His knee tweaked something horrible, but he tried to ignore it. Now wasn't the time. He glugged at his bottle of water and then threw his towel at the ball boy.

One more point to victory. He had to do this.

Everything flashed across his mind, his daughter's school fees, his gambling debts and an increasingly expensive mistress. He needed to win the series and take the money. Already, he'd agreed that if he failed, he'd slit his wrists.

It wasn't worth living through the disgrace of a bankrupt veteran.

Harold padded his way back to the baseline. Faced up to Guerrero, on the other side of the net. Guerrero's long, dark hair was creased to his head with a sweatband, while sweat glued the loose strands to his cheeks.

Waiting to receive the serve, Harold swayed back and forth.

Eyes fixed on the yellow ball.

Guerrero leaped and whacked the ball back.

The ball bounced into the service box, then sailed upwards, whistling past Harold's ear and thudding into the advertising hoarding behind.

"Shit!" Harold cried out, accepting the towel from the ball boy and then he wiped his hands.

Damn the heat, it was throwing him off.

The scoreboard now reading 6-5 they changed ends.

Harold needed to get back in the zone.

Concentrate, Godammit.

Guerrero threw up the ball and Harold lost it in the sun. It whipped past him. A *buzz* announced that it had struck the net cord on the way over. A let.

Almost without hesitation, Guerrero hit his next serve. It fizzled past Harold, striking the rim of his racquet.

The crowd roared and Harold accepted the balls.

6-6

Harold's heart beat faster. He threw up the ball. Hit it. Into the net. Second service. His knee burned in pain. He bounced the ball a couple of times, wondering whether Guerrero had the same high-stakes resting on this game. No doubt he just wanted the joy of beating him, if only he knew. Picturing that smug grin of Guerrero's, Harold put all his power into the shot. The ball whistled over, catching the rim of the service box and jumping up at Guerrero.

Guerrero whipped it back.

Somehow, Harold wrestled his racquet round the ball and returned it.

Guerrero skidded across the ground, on his knees. The ball thumped into the backboard.

Harold let loose an enormous, "Yes!" with an accompanying fist-pump.

7-6

Match point.

Guerrero remained on the ground. His shoulders rising and falling in rapid motion.

Harold accepted the next ball and bounced it impatiently. He wanted to clinch this one and turn his mind to the deciding match, which would take place tomorrow.

A physiotherapist jumped out onto the court and crouched down alongside Guerrero.

A sinister thought crossed Harold's mind. What if Guerrero couldn't continue? He'd have to forfeit . . . and Harold would take the money.

Guerrero got to his feet and shook his legs.

Harold glanced to the umpire. "Are we going to be here all night, or what?"

With a shrug, the umpire tapped his wrist—indicating he was timing the interruption.

Guerrero continued talking to the physio, who gave him a pill and a bottle of water.

Harold dropped his racquet and ball in protest. He called over to Guerrero. "Hey, you gonna give me some of that, or what?" Then he stamped up to the umpire. "Are you letting this pass?"

"Calm down, please," the umpire said. "They're approved. Nothing for you to worry about."

Harold shook his head and marched back to the baseline. It never paid off to argue, not in the end. Action was the only answer. He muttered to himself, "If he grows goddamn biceps and pummels me down the line . . ."

Guerrero danced on his mark and raised his racquet, to signal he was ready.

Harold threw up the ball and smashed a magnificent ace. He raised his arms in recognition of the crowd and soaked up the applause.

1-1 with one match to play in the three-match series.

Harold was still in with a chance.

As was characteristic of their rivalry, they forewent the handshake. Guerrero strolled over to his chair, picked up his bags and stormed off to the changing rooms.

After signing a few autographs, Harold followed.

2

HAROLD took a brief shower and wrapped a towel round himself. When he emerged, Guerrero was already dressed in a pair of smart trousers. His hairy black chest exposed, he applied a roll-on deodorant.

Sneering, Harold approached. "What was all that pill stuff about?"

"Nothing to do with you."

"If it's an energy supplement we should both get it, don't you think?"

On the bench beside Guerrero, Harold noticed the bottle of pills. He swiped for it.

Guerrero knocked his hand away. "None of your business!"

Harold's nerves fizzed. He was of half a mind to knock Guerrero out. If he hadn't needed the money from winning tomorrow's game, he probably would have.

Guerrero wiped his neck with his towel and sighed. "All right, take a look if you want."

One eye fixed on him, Harold snatched up the pills. He inspected the label.

"They're for my heart," Guerrero said.

Harold glanced at him.

"That's right, I have a heart condition." Guerrero whipped them from Harold's hand and dropped them in his sports bag, before he had a chance to fully absorb the information on the label.

"And you're sure the Association cleared them?" Harold said.

"Yes." Guerrero chucked a jumper round his shoulders and buttoned up. After a quick look in the mirror, he slung his bag over his shoulder. "I'd like to stay and chat all night, but, you know, I've got this nice piece waiting for me at the hotel."

"Shouldn't you wait till tomorrow, before celebrating?"

Guerrero chuckled. "I'm gonna cream you. Don't think I didn't notice your gammy knee. You practically hobbled through the third set."

A twinge ran up Harold's spine. He hated it when his opponents noticed his weaknesses.

Guerrero hesitated when he reached the door of the changing room. "Hear you've had some financial problems recently."

"Yeah, well," Harold said. "That's all paper talk. I wouldn't pay attention to it."

"Still, no smoke without fire." Guerrero inspected his nails. "Know what I'm going to do with the five million?"

"What?"

"I'm going to burn it. Right there in the middle of the court." Guerrero flashed a bright-white smile and strutted out.

Harold cursed him. He put his clothes out ready and dried himself. The only way to wipe that grin off Guerrero's face was to beat him.

How had he let his knee show? What an amateur! He'd always prided himself on his ability to hide injury. Perhaps Guerrero knew him too well. They'd fought too many times out on the court.

Was Guerrero getting inside his head?

Had he *already* got inside his head?

But those pills . . . a warped and devious plan formed in his mind.

On his way out, Harold passed the umpire—dressed in a white suit. Word had it that Trevor Purvis was paying the umpire over a million for the series. As a documented official, he gave the series an extra layer of credibility.

Harold stopped the umpire to chat. "Good game today, eh?"

"Congratulations on your victory. Should be an interesting climax tomorrow."

"Say, what's the chance of rain for tomorrow?"

"Oh, I'd say it's pretty certain."

Harold's eyes narrowed. "How certain?"

"Sixty, seventy percent."

"Shame."

The umpire sighed and inspected his shirt cuffs. "Yes, tends to break up the game doesn't it?"

"Well, I'll leave you to your evening."

"Thanks." The umpire grinned and slapped Harold on the shoulder. "Well played and good luck for the match."

Harold watched the umpire stroll down to the reception, no doubt going to meet up with some expensive escort girl . . . or *boy*, it was hard to tell where these high-class officials hung their hats.

3

THE NEXT DAY, Harold hoisted one leg up on the bench and strapped up his knee. He was fresh and ready to grind Guerrero into the ground.

Guerrero strolled in, still wearing sunglasses. Today he had a black, shiny suit on. He truly thought he was going to win, didn't he?

Harold winced. "Oof, this knee's really coming apart these days."

Laying a hand on his shoulder, Guerrero pulled down his shades. "Time to pass the torch, eh, old man?"

Strapped up, Harold stretched. "Not quite, I reckon there's at least one more match left in this mongrel."

"Keep telling yourself that. You know, if you really want, I'll write you out a check for your debts. I can afford it, after all."

Harold stepped up to him, chest pushed out. "I told you that's all hearsay. Don't believe it."

"Suit yourself, but maybe it'd help you concentrate on the match. I'd never be able to focus if I felt a sword hanging over me."

"Some of us are better adapted to pressure, that's all."

"Well, we'll see about that today. Out on court."

Harold stepped away and picked up his bag. He marched out onto the court. The crowd cheered and he clapped his hands over his head to acknowledge them.

Dark clouds loomed above, ready to rain down.

If it got any darker, they might need the floodlights.

Sitting down in his chair and taking a swig of water, Harold thought about how this might very well be his last match. All the majors he'd won, he had nothing left to prove. By all rights he should've been in his Spanish villa, feet up beside the pool. It was

170

a shame he'd let life get on top of him, all those added bonuses had added up and now threatened to crush him.

When Guerrero emerged, every member of the crowd got to their feet and applauded. The closer he got to the chairs, the louder the screams got.

Did they love him more?

Harold shook his head. Sometimes he was his own worst enemy—the first to write himself off. He gripped his racquet and hopped out onto the court for the warm up.

The ball boy handed him three balls, he selected the best-looking two. Squeezing the soft yellow fuzz in his left hand, he swooped back his racquet in his right—meeting the ball at the top of his motion.

A satisfying *thwack!* shook his racquet strings and the ball skimmed over the line of the opposing service box. Once he'd hit a dozen or so serves, he felt good about himself.

No doubt about it, today he was on top of his game.

Still dressed in his tracksuit top, Guerrero took up his place on the opposite baseline and hit his own serves.

Harold watched a few, mesmerised. It was true what the pundits said. Guerrero really did have the most elegant serve in the game.

Shaking his head, Harold tried to break out of his admiration.

'Get out of the bubble and into the zone,' an ex-coach's words reverberated round his brain.

Harold jumped up and down then fired another serve across.

It narrowly missed Guerrero, who sneered back at him.

The portly umpire waddled up the ladder to his chair and spoke into his microphone.

"Time."

Harold returned to his chair and wiped his face with the towel. After a swig of water, he was good to go. He sprinted to the baseline and received the first few balls. He'd serve first today.

Guerrero inched out onto the court, his head bowed and mouth moving.

Often, Harold wondered what that was all about. Guerrero always muttered words to himself, like some kind of prayer.

Harold shook his head and grinned. Some people loved to make others responsible—some *god*, or whatever—that was a weakness he had to exploit.

Heart pounding, Harold threw the ball into the air. It bolted over the net. Guerrero returned to mid-court and Harold sent a belter down the tramlines.

The audience roared.

15 – Love

Warmth built in the pit of Harold's stomach. He looked up to the stands.

No Trevor Purvis yet.

Unbelievable.

All the money he'd spent on this game and he didn't even want to watch from start to finish. Perhaps his helicopter pilot had taken one look at the clouds and advised him to take the limo. It made sense. Traffic was terrible at this time. No matter. Harold would get Guerrero on the ropes.

Surely Trevor would show up for the grandstand finish.

Harold spat and threw up the ball. This time he imagined Guerrero's face on the ball. He sent it into the corner of the serving box. Guerrero tumbled head over heel. His racquet clattered across the court. The audience gasped and Harold hid his chuckle with his towel.

30 – Love

Grimacing, Guerrero dusted himself down and got to his feet. He hobbled over to his mark and waited.

Not giving him any time to settle, Harold flicked over the

next serve. Guerrero returned, almost catching Harold off-balance. With a deep breath, Harold slammed his heel into the ground and changed direction, catching the ball on his strings. It trickled over the net sending Guerrero, huffing and puffing, across court.

However, when he arrived, it had already bounced twice.

Harold straightened up and received the next ball. He called over the net, "Gonna have to get your skates on, pal!"

Guerrero glowered.

40 – Love

Was there a note of admiration in the umpire's voice? He looked up to the chair and the umpire smirked.

Someone got laid last night.

The last serve slipped out of Harold. His second ace of the match and he took the first game. He sidled up the net, racquet in hand.

Guerrero was red-faced and sweat poured down his cheeks.

"Everything all right?" Harold said. "You look knackered."

"I'm fine."

Seeing his eyes, Harold realised why Guerrero had worn sunglasses into the changing room that morning. He had enormous bags under his eyes. Clearly he'd been out the night before. What *cheek*. Harold was going to teach him a lesson today, the arrogant sod.

Guerrero accepted his lot of balls and strolled over to the baseline.

The first set flew by and Harold took it six to love.

They sat alongside one another in their chairs. Each sipping at their bottles of water.

Guerrero chucked a damp towel over his head and bent over himself.

He looked like he might be sick.

"How're you getting on, champ?" Harold said.

". . . Fine."

"How about we make things interesting, seeing as this money doesn't matter to you?"

Guerrero's towel twitched.

"Double or nothing?"

Guerrero shook his head. "You don't have the money to lose."

"Does it really look like you're going to win today?"

"I never give less than one-hundred percent."

Harold put his bottle down and jumped to his feet. "Time's wasting. Let's get this thing over with. Do we have a deal?"

Guerrero threw off the towel and leaped up. He held out his hand. "Absolutely."

They shook on it.

The second set was much harder work for Harold.

In truth, Guerrero had him running all over. When they reached 3 – 3, Harold breathed a sigh of relief and collapsed into his chair.

Guerrero said, "I'm sure Trevor will let you quit, while you're ahead."

Harold shook his head and panted. "I'll. Show. You." He gulped down his water and glanced over his shoulder.

Guerrero placed his bottle down. "That's right, not even here yet. And they say I'm arrogant."

People in the crowd chattered amongst themselves.

Harold turned his head to see Trevor Purvis channel his way up to the executive box. His smile shone even from where he sat. Trevor waved to them and, as if hypnotised, Harold waved back.

Trevor held up a transparent bag of money.

A block of green.

Harold's stomach churned.

At least Trevor had decided to show up.

They played on into a tiebreak, which Guerrero won 6 – 3. It left the game at one set each.

Harold returned to his seat and chucked his racquet down.

He was blowing it—and didn't he know it.

"Sure you don't want to take up my offer?" Guerrero said. "I'll even give you the prize money."

Harold glared at him. Never in his life had he taken charity and he wasn't going to start now. Not when he was approaching middle-age and was supposed to be an adult.

Trying to get his mind out of a losing mentality, he stared at a spot in mid-air and let all his responsibilities come back to him. Last night one of the loan sharks had called him up and demanded a payment there and then. When he'd told him he was out of the country, the shark had threatened his family. Once he'd won the match, he'd snatch up the cash and sprint to the airport. He didn't want to mess these people round anymore. If everything went according to plan today, he wouldn't need to.

"Time!" the umpire called.

Harold picked out a new racquet, ripped off the plastic and strolled out onto the court.

Clouds piled in over the stadium and the floodlights flickered on.

Harold eyed Guerrero's service arc and then watched the ball onto his strings, where it bounced off into the net.

Harold's concentration was gone and he knew it.

Harold glanced up at the executive box and then at the sky, praying.

Halfway through the final set, Guerrero led him four games to nothing. Some members of the crowd shouted things, and the buzz increased as anticipation rose at the end coming into view.

Harold took up his mark and bounced the ball. A spot of rain fell on him. He hesitated and looked to the umpire, who remained still.

He hit the serve and lost yet another point. Rain fell harder and soon it was a shower.

Heart in mouth, Harold observed the umpire lean over his microphone.

"Play suspended."

Ball boys rushed the court, collapsing the net.

Harold dashed off to the changing rooms. His mind was split. On the one hand, he felt delighted about the chance to regroup but, on the other, he was scared stiff of the idea that had been swarming about at the back of his head.

Over his shoulder, an army of stewards pulled covers onto the court.

Guerrero took his time packing up at his chair. For all his success today, Harold had no doubt he was struggling with fatigue. His face was dark-red, like yesterday. He would teach him a lesson about respect—one which might cost Guerrero his life.

4

ALONE IN THE DRESSING ROOM, Harold dumped his racquets and bounded over to Guerrero's bag. He unzipped and scrabbled about inside. His hand rested on the bottle of pills, which he withdrew.

He examined the label.

Couldn't pronounce the name, even in his head.

Without another moment's thought, he hopped over to the sink and tipped the contents down the plughole. Once he was sure there was nothing left, he crossed the room, dropped the emptied bottle back inside Guerrero's bag and sat back on the bench tightening his knee support.

Guerrero strutted in with a slimy grin. "How's the knee holding up?"

"Not too bad, but might have to take it easy for the rest of the game."

Guerrero sat down alongside his bag. "This is only a shower —I have to assure you the respite is temporary."

Harold eyed him as he searched through his bag for the bottle.

When Guerrero withdrew it, he held it in his hand and gestured at him. "Got kids?"

"What?"

"Do you have any kids?"

"A daughter. I'm sure you've seen the pictures in the paper."

Guerrero unscrewed the cap.

Harold's guts twinged.

"Nope, I never read that rubbish, believe it or not." Guerrero looked inside the bottle and frowned. His face lost all colour.

"What's the matter?"

Guerrero stared at him.

Would he attack him?

Instead, Guerrero replaced the cap and dropped his bottle back inside his bag and zipped up. "Nothing. It's just, you know, kids. Ridiculous. My youngest kept me up all night."

"Really?"

"Yes, my wife's been a little poorly recently too. So responsibility's all fallen on me. "

Harold's heart skipped a beat. Perhaps Guerrero wasn't the libertine he'd built him up as. "Sure you didn't sneak out for a couple of drinks?"

Guerrero snorted. "I wish."

For the rest of the rain break, they sat in silence. Harold swum in his thoughts. What should he do? Guerrero knew he didn't have his heart pills, but did he realise it was Harold who'd chucked them? For the first time in their long rivalry, he realised he was empathising with Guerrero. He remembered his own daughter keeping him up all night.

God, he'd got so angry with his wife about it.

He directly blamed her when he got knocked out of a ranking competition.

Harold glanced at Guerrero. Was it just him, or had he taken on a darker colour? What would happen if he didn't get his pills? He ran various situations through his mind.

The ambulance outside the stadium, they'd get to him and administer whatever he needed—surely.

Guerrero would be fine, and the series would be forfeited . . . Harold would win by default . . . but what if it all went wrong?

It wasn't worth thinking about. Harold needed the money. It was as simple as that. And there was no way he'd ever win unless he forced Guerrero to retire, but through any means?

On the point of telling Guerrero he'd disposed of his pills, the umpire entered the dressing room. "Rain's let off, gentlemen. If you'd come out for the restart."

Guerrero got up and bounced toward the exit. "Let's finish this, then."

Harold remained on the bench a few moments, considering what might be about to unfold. He snatched up his racquet and gripped it tight in his hand—determined to win.

It was him or Guerrero.

One of them might die today.

5

THE CROWD applauded the players as they emerged onto the court. Harold clapped his racquet and felt hot blood rushing through his veins.

This was it, his day of reckoning.

He needed that money.

Harold resumed his serve, which he lost in record time.

5 – 0

Guerrero was serving for the match now. He padded round the net for the changeover, narrowing his eyes when he passed Harold.

Harold bounced to his mark, trying to forget that his life was about to end.

But, right then, the crowd let out a long *ooh* sound.

Harold spun round.

On the other side of the net, Guerrero lay face down.

Medics rushed out to him.

Harold felt intensely self-conscious. What should he do to appear natural? He wandered round the net, standing back and putting on his best look of concern.

Men swarmed round Guerrero. Through the melee, he noticed one of them pumping his chest—administering CPR. He wandered closer and peeked over them.

Guerrero lay quite still, face red, eyes closed, lips slightly parted.

Was he dead?

Someone put their arm round Harold's shoulders and led him away. He glanced behind. It was the umpire. "Come on. We'd better give them some space."

They walked off toward the tunnel. Members of the crowd

stood, trying to see what was happening. One of them called out to him, "Hey, Harold! What's going on?"

Unable to speak, Harold shrugged.

6

THE UMPIRE sat down alongside Harold in the dressing room. Together, they waited for news.

Finally, after about half an hour, Guerrero's coach appeared. He had a sombre look about him. He crouched down on his haunches. "I've got bad news."

Harold peered at him, doing his best to appear shocked.

"Guerrero's passed away."

Harold nodded and then the tears erupted from his ducts, running down his cheeks. The umpire pulled him into his chest and the coach reached out and touched him on the knee. "We've got some grief councillors on the way. They'll help you get through it. Remember, it wasn't your fault. It was just a coincidence."

Though Harold couldn't help but feel the tension building up in his chest, neither could he stop the words tumbling out, ". . . What about the money?"

"Mm, I don't know." The coach exchanged glances with the umpire. "I presume it'll go to you—officially it counts as a forfeit."

Harold sobbed. "Sorry, I don't know what's going through my mind. Everything's such a mess."

"I know, I understand."

The coach hung there a few moments and then patted Harold on the knee, before pacing out the changing room and back to the court.

"Do you need anything?" the umpire said.

"I'd like to be alone, if that's okay."

"Of course," the umpire said, getting up to leave.

As Harold heard the footsteps disappear, the umpire leaving, he felt a smile creep across his face. He clenched his fists.

His greatest victory?

7

A WEEK LATER, back home in his country mansion, the doorbell rang.

Harold padded down the stairs still in his slippers and dressing gown. That morning, the money had been deposited in his account. All his problems were solved.

He opened the door to a pair of suited men. One was small and stocky, while the other was thin and tall.

His heart skipped a beat and the smile slipped from his face. He'd paid everything off.

What did they want now?

"Good morning, sir," the stocky one said. "Name's Detective Peterson, this is my associate Detective Morgan. We'd like to ask you a couple of questions, if we may."

Harold grimaced. "Really? This isn't a good time." He attempted to shut the door, but Detective Morgan stuck his well-polished shoe in the gap.

Peterson stepped inside and grabbed his wrist. "We've seen the CCTV footage from the dressing room, sir. I think you'd better come with us."

"No!" Harold wriggled from his grasp and ran into his house.

Both policemen pursued him, upstairs and into his bedroom.

Harold climbed up to the third floor and emerged onto the balcony.

A breeze blew his dressing gown up round his body. He stepped over to the edge and looked out at the concrete below. It would be a quick death.

When he looked back, he saw the men hesitate at the door. Peterson called out, "Sir, step away from the ledge."

Harold closed his eyes and vaulted over.

NIGEL

1

THE SCREAMS ERUPTING from the cave rattled Jens's bones. He stamped on his cigarette and ran back inside. After about fifty feet, Jens had to crawl to avoid the low ceiling. His head hit something hard and he collapsed. Jens rubbed his temples.

Heider's egg-white eyes pierced the darkness. "Cave in! Nigel's trapped!"

They worked to pull the rocks off Nigel—they had to reach him before he stopped breathing. Black dirt covered Jens's hands and his lungs filled with heavy dust. He glimpsed a flash of white. Skin. He grabbed the torch from his back pocket.

The small circle of light settled on Nigel's face. His eyes were closed.

Jens snatched Heider's shirt. "Come on! We've almost got him!" Jens heaved rocks off Nigel's body. Once he'd cleared enough, he took Nigel's feet then shouted to Heider, "Take that side!"

Heider seized Nigel's shoulders and, in their crouched position, they dragged Nigel toward the cave entrance.

The sun beat down on their filthy bodies. Jens watched on as Heider pumped Nigel's chest. Heider paused then squeezed Nigel's nose. He blew air into his mouth. Nothing happened. Nigel's arms remained lifeless at his sides.

An enormous *crash* came from inside the cave and a few rocks tumbled out.

Heider looked up. "Shit! That could've been us."

Jens took Nigel's hand—the first time he'd ever touched his friend like that, so different from the rough handshakes and *slaps* on the back. The tenderness overwhelmed him. He wanted to cry.

Heider held his fingers to Nigel's neck then shook his head.

A jolt of fear ran up Jens's spine and hot tears ran down his face. He glanced at Nigel's face, his blue cheeks, dust-covered lips, and eyes staring into the void.

Heider got to his feet, paused to light a cigarette, and then went round the corner.

Jens's brain rang out like an echo chamber, remembering he was responsible—he'd brought them here. Indeed, he'd thought independent mining was novel. They would get out with sacks of raw material then head off for some fun in the sun—respite from their empty and prospect-less lives. He'd never thought it would cost him his friend. What the hell were they going to do?

2

THE WIND PICKED UP and clouds spotted the clear blue sky. The weather here was like a pendulum, swinging back and forth from one extreme to the next.

Heider came round the corner. "Still dead?"

Jens wiped away a tear, taking Heider's matter-of-fact way of speaking to be shock. "What do we do now?"

Heider stepped closer. "We should bury him."

Jens shook his head and stood up. His knees ached from crouching. "We should take him back to his family. Go to the village. Find a car."

Heider looked out across the valley. His glassy eyes reflected the sun. He shrugged. "Whatever, I want to get back to my girlfriend."

Jens sympathised, he wanted to get back to his family—away from this horrible situation. Jens sidled up to Heider and laid his hand on his shoulder. "Let's get the tents packed up."

Heider picked Nigel up under his armpits. Nigel's head flopped down onto his chest. They each propped up a shoulder, like carrying a deceased soldier from battle.

Every so often Heider had to stop to cough. All Jens's fault too. Heider must've inhaled a lot of dust in the mine. And for what? Between them they had a sprinkling of dust—probably enough raw material between them to buy a half pint.

Jens tripped on a loose rock and fell. Gravel bit at his kneecaps and the sharp pain rattled his nerves. When he looked up, he saw Nigel hanging from Heider's arms like a ragdoll.

On his hands and knees, Jens wanted to cry again. The shock and pain of the fall had sharpened his senses.

"Come on!" Heider said. "I'm going to drop him."

Jens got up and brushed himself down. When he looked to

the village, he realised how far they had to go. Walking up to the mine had taken the best part of six hours—half a day. No telling how long it would take with a dead body.

After assuming his position on Nigel's left, Jens pondered the unnatural and horrific feel of live skin on dead. Grandfathers, grandmothers, uncles and aunts—all those funerals he'd been to and felt nothing. Different this time. Death was up close and personal. Close enough to whisper in his ear.

Above their heads, black clouds gathered and the rain came down. Jens ignored the first light drops, determined to get down to the village and sort out their situation. Heider seemed to feel the same, walking faster. Jens estimated they had a good five hours between them and the village and just a couple hours of sunlight. Walking in the dark was one thing, but walking in the dark under pounding rain—with enormous cliffs on either side of the path—was stupid.

Jens adjusted his grip. "Heid?"

Heider walked onward through the drizzle.

"Heid? We've got to stop for the night. This won't let up 'til tomorrow."

Heider surveyed the path. "I guess you're right."

Jens put Nigel's weight on Heider then pulled off his backpack. He unzipped the top. His hands were damp and shivered as he reached for the items inside. He dropped the tent poles onto the ground.

Up ahead, low grey clouds covered the village—certainly the right decision to stop for the night. A night in a tent with a corpse. A shudder passed through Jens and goose bumps clutched at his shirt.

3

JENS LAID OUT the sleeping bags inside the tent. They put Nigel's body in between the two of them. No-one should have to snuggle up against a dead body alone.

Rain tapped away at the canvas and the electric lantern swung back-and-forth from the roof, sending every shadow into an epileptic dance. Jens noticed the deep veiny-blue circle on Nigel's forehead, where he supposed the fatal rock had struck him.

Jens thought about when his father had asked him if he wanted to take part in his grandfather's vigil. He was about fifteen at the time. His father told him it would mean a lot to his grandfather's memory, because he specified precisely in his will that he wanted his grandsons to look over him. Jens remembered thinking how stupid it was and laughed out of hand. The expression on his father's face had stopped him dead. It was then he realised that when people talked about memories, they were really talking about what was inside living and breathing people. Not really spiritual at all, more like vanity—like a survey conducted to find out how much other people really cared about their loved one.

Jens had said 'No.' He hadn't seen the point. Not for his father. Not for anyone. Until now.

Heider lay on his side, facing away from Jens. Was he asleep? It seemed impossible.

Jens coughed. "Heid?"

Heider groaned.

"Are you asleep?"

"Nah . . . Can't."

Jens waited him to say something else, but he didn't. Jens's hands shook. "Isn't it weird?"

191

"What?"

"You know? Lying here with him, I mean, what usually happens when someone dies?"

Heider didn't reply.

Jens continued, "I suppose the ambulance comes, or the undertaker. People probably leave the body alone, then—"

Heider rolled over to face Jens in the darkness. "All right, that's enough. Let's go to sleep."

"But you're not going to be able to sleep."

Heider snorted. "Might as well try," then, quieter, "Never sleep without my girlfriend."

4

IN THE MORNING, the sun's rays crept up the canvas and illuminated their outlines. Nigel's body remained between them. His hands rested across his chest in a cross. Jens had put him like that. He supposed he'd seen it on TV or something. The air reeked.

Jens sniffed. He reached over Nigel and tapped Heider. "You up?"

Heider stirred. ". . . Yeah."

"Shall we get going?"

Heider sat up in his sleeping bag and rubbed his face. He had deep black circles under his eyes.

After rolling up their sleeping bags and mats, they came to move Nigel. Jens reached out to touch him. Ice ran through his veins and he froze. Something deep inside him prevented him crossing the gap and making contact with Nigel's skin.

"What's wrong?" Heider said.

Jens stared at his fingers—willing them to touch the body. But, they wouldn't.

"Come on." Heider lifted his side of the body. "Jesus! It's like a block of ice. Rock hard!"

Jens clutched his hands to his chest. "I can't do it."

"What?" Heider creased his forehead. "Just don't think about it."

"I don't know what's wrong with me."

Heider sighed then dragged the body from the tent. "I'll look after Nigel. You put the rest of the stuff away."

Jens trembled. It was one thing to carry a fresh dead body, but one in the clutches of *rigor mortis* was something else.

Once Jens had packed the equipment, he got over his fear

and helped to carry the body. They made their way down the slope without speaking.

5

WELL INTO THE VALLEY, perhaps forty minutes from the village, Heider spoke. "When we get to the village, what'll we do?"

"Find a doctor, I guess." Jens shrugged his backpack down onto the road to give his shoulders a rest.

"But he's dead."

Jens shook his head. "I don't know, I thought that's what you're supposed to do when someone dies. Get a doctor. Perhaps there'll be an inquest."

Heider eyeballed Jens. "I was thinking. We really should just bury him out here."

Jens frowned. "What? Why have we come all this way, when we could've dug a hole at the pit?"

"You didn't want to."

"And I don't want to now." Jens removed a bottle of water and took a swig.

"I mean, we're his best friends, right?"

"Yeah."

"And, Nigel always told us how much he hated his family and how much they hated him. So, why shouldn't it be us who puts him in the ground?"

Jens squinted in the bright sunlight. "It's not just that, though, Heid, there's legal tape."

Heider's mouth turned down at the corners. "What if they say we committed murder?"

"What? What are you talking about?"

"You know, we were the only witnesses."

Jens shrugged. "We don't have anything to hide." He put the bottle away and zipped up the rucksack. "Come on, let's go to the village and get it over with. We're just making it worse for ourselves, waiting out here until it starts raining again."

They continued on down the road.

6

WHEN THEY REACHED the village, people sat on their porches, looking out from their storefronts. No-one said anything, only their silent eyes watching them pass by.

A tingle ran up Jens's spine and the cobbled streets wobbled under his feet. He glanced at Heider. Nothing. Heider kept walking, Nigel's arm propped over his shoulder. Jens walked on—he didn't want to ask the people here.

Two market stalls stood in the main square. One sold salted fish and the other grey fruits. In the background, a huge medieval-style church dominated the skyline—the spire reaching up to the heavens. They needed to ask someone or else they'd just keep going until they came out the other side of the village.

Jens went up to the man selling fish. "Excuse me?"

The man's bushy black eyebrows remained level with his empty blue eyes. He wore a white apron covered in yellow and black stains, while underneath he had a blue and red checked shirt. In his hand, he held an enormous cleaver.

"It's my friend." Jens sobbed. "He's dead."

The man stood with his cleaver hanging in the air.

"Please?"

The old man glanced at Nigel's body. "Come with me." He laid the cleaver down then turned to the woman selling grey fruits. "Watch the stall, will you?"

She didn't respond—staring into space as her hands shelled the fruits.

A buzz, like an electric shock, passed through Jens's veins. He didn't like this place. Something wasn't right about it.

Heider kept his eyes to the ground, Nigel resting against his shoulder.

7

THE MAN LED THEM DOWN a crooked side street. He stopped outside a door and removed a key from his jean pocket.

The room was small and stank of fish. In one corner, a table and chairs awaited them while, in the other was the man's bed. Dust covered oil paintings hung off the walls at fifteen degree angles. Beyond, the kitchen and—what Jens presumed to be—the door leading to the bathroom.

The man tugged the light cord and a one-hundred watt bulb chased away the darkness. "Put the body on the table."

Jens nodded at Heider, who took a deep breath. They hefted the solid body into the air. Jens's grip slipped and the body landed with a dull *thud*.

The man's eyes darted from one to the other. "Want a drink, boys?"

Heider sank into one of the chairs. "Yeah."

The man disappeared into the kitchen. Pots and pans clattered. He re-emerged clutching three glasses and a bottle of whiskey. He handed Heider and Jens a glass each. The freezing cup reminded Jens of Nigel's skin.

They clinked glasses and took a drink.

The man grimaced. "Hell! Been a long time since I saw a corpse here, in the village." The man looked at Nigel's body. "Used to happen all the time when the men still worked the mine." The man chuckled. "Well, suppose you guys are looking for a lift into town."

Heider eyed Jens. "That's right."

"Afraid the next lift'll be with the cattle truck in the morning."

Jens watched the man refill his glass. "No-one has a truck for hire?"

The man looked at Jens. "As you boys know, takes about two hours of driving to get back to town." He shook his head. "No chance of you boys getting a lift back tonight. People here go there then turn right round and come back. No time to do that now and it doesn't make sense to drive all night—not on these roads." The man blew the dust from the bottle and examined the label. "Anyway, I'm really sorry about your friend."

Heider bowed his head. "Yeah, well. These things happen, I guess." Heider accepted the next shot—tilting his glass toward the man. Before Jens knew it, the man was refilling his glass too.

8

AFTER THE FIFTH SHOT, the man gave the bottle to Heider and made to leave. "Gotta shut up shop for the day. Make yourself at home, boys. Shower's through there." He wobbled his way across the room then paused in the door frame. "Better cover up your mate. There's a sheet in the cupboard above the bed." He slammed the door.

After another shot, Heider slammed his glass down on the table and got up from the chair. "I'm going to take a shower."

The whiskey pumped round Jens's veins. "What did you mean, 'these things happen?'"

Heider rifled through the bag. "Nothing, just it was unfortunate." Heider looked up. "Look, man, I'm just as cut up about Nigel as you, really. You know? It's all like a nightmare. Maybe I'm in shock." He shrugged. "You look like you are too, perhaps you should lie down. I can get out your sleeping bag, if you want." Heider unclipped the sleeping mat from the rucksack and it dropped to the floor. He tossed the sleeping bag at Jens.

Jens caught it.

"Here you go, dude. Have a rest."

"Thanks." Jens laid out the sleeping bag then went across to the wardrobe. He removed the folded white sheet and draped it over Nigel.

Jens lay down with his hands tucked behind his head as a pillow. He listened to Heider move about the bathroom. The tap squeaked and water dripped down.

Heider screamed.

Jens shuddered then propped himself up on his elbows. The water continued. Jens got to his feet and rapped on the wooden door. "Heid? You all right in there?"

"Water's fucking freezing!"

Jens exhaled. "You're all right then?"

"What are you, my girlfriend?" Heider paused. "Freezing my bollocks off, but apart from that . . ."

Jens returned to his sleeping bag.

9

LATER ON, the doorknob rattled and the door jerked open. The man stumbled in. "Getting some rest?" he said to Jens.

"Yeah."

The man's eyes seemed to flash. "Up you come, laddie! Whenever we lost someone down the mine, we'd drink all night!"

Jens's stomach turned over. He could've done with food or rest, instead of more whiskey. He got up from the sleeping bag.

The man knocked back another drink. "I'm going to get a stew on. Come and chat with me in the kitchen, not often I get company in the evenings. Not since the wife passed."

With a final look to the bathroom door, Jens followed the man.

10

WATER BOILED on the stove and a large slab of meat bled crimson onto the counter. The cleaver lay to one side.

The man chopped his way through the vegetables. "What happened?"

Jens leant against the counter and reeled through the story. The man listened intently, but never looked up from his chopping.

Once Jens had finished, the man brushed the vegetables into the pot. "Bit weird, ain't it?"

"What?"

The man made a face. "It's just, you go in and your mate's coming out the other way."

In the bathroom, the water continued to run.

"He was getting away from the cave in."

"How long did it take to dig your friend out?"

"About ten minutes."

"It's just." The man paused and looked to the bathroom. "About twenty years ago a very similar thing happened."

Jens leant closer to the man.

"Two young boys from the village went up the mountain and only one came back." He eyed Jens. "He ran down the mountain screaming, saying there'd been a cave in." The man tilted his head. "Well, when the men dug the rocks from his body, they didn't see any sign of a cave in." He pointed to the ceiling with the cleaver. "The roof formation was too secure. What they did find, however, was a bruise on the boy's head." The man dropped a few slices of meat into the pot. "Just like the one on your mate."

The water stopped running in the bathroom and soggy foot-steps came from the main room. Heider walked into the kitchen a towel wrapped round him. "Smells good!"

11

A FTER DINNER they ploughed on with the drinking—smashing their glasses together and making headway through the bottle. Their shot glasses made wet rings inches from Nigel's body. Jens tried to shrug off the effects of the alcohol. The man had put him on his guard.

The man squinted, holding up his glass. "Now! It's time for each of you to tell a story about Nigel. *You!*" He pointed to Heider.

Jens's heart leapt to his throat. He didn't want Heider to guess they'd been talking about him in the kitchen, speculating.

Heider put down his glass and shook his head.

"Wha?" The old man's arm waivered, still holding the glass.

Heider stared at the man. "I don't want to."

"But it's tradition!" The man smiled. His words echoed around the room. Silence followed. The old man raised his bushy eyebrows then turned to Jens. "All right, how about you?"

"Me?" Although an obvious turn of events, it took Jens off-guard. He didn't have a story prepared. He racked his brains. "When we were about fifteen, in school." Jens paused, already tears tugged at his eyes. "I remember one day after registration. Us three snuck out through a hole in the bushes, near the school gate."

Did Heider have a faint smile on his face?

Jens continued, "We did it quite a lot, perhaps three or four times a month. Anyway, this time it was different. We went to get fish and chips from the local shop, a late breakfast. On the way there, we laughed and joked. I don't know what we talked about. We came out with our packets of chips and Nigel told us he wanted to go to the bank, across the road. It happened in slow motion, I don't know if he wasn't watching the road, or what, but he walked out onto the tarmac and, next thing we know, there's screeching tyres and Nigel's lying on his back."

Heider smiled.

The old man leant in on his crooked elbows.

"Me and Heid just stood there, like this." Jens dropped his jaw. "Because it was a narrow road, people were already beeping their horns trying to get past. Then the driver got out of the car. Our Deputy Head!"

Heider chuckled and shook his head.

"He was this great big monster of a guy and, I swear, the first thing I thought was, *He's going to kill Nigel.*' However, he bent down, while me and Heid hid our faces, and brought Nigel to his feet. He brushed him down then led him back across the road, like a little old lady! The best part was when he saw me and Heid. The look on his face!" Jens shook his head. "Handed us fifty quid and told us not to tell anyone. Got back in his car and shot off!"

Heider looked into his glass. "Poor bastard."

The old man eyed Heider. "And what happened at school, he never said anything?"

Jens wiped off the tears of joy. "Nah. Couldn't, could he? They fenced up the hole by the gate soon after. Didn't really matter, though, we were out of there in six months."

The man thumped his fist on the table. "More drink!"

Jens got up from his chair, balancing himself with the back of his chair. "I'm going to turn in, I think."

"Suit yourself." The old man refilled his glass. "You've said your piece." He turned on Heider. "You, however, have not."

Snug in his sleeping bag, Jens lay back and tried to sleep. The old man and Heider murmured to each other across the table. Every so often, Jens thought one of them had fallen asleep face down on the table. Then, after a period of silence, the other would continue the conversation. The last time Jens glanced at the table only a dribble of whiskey remained in the bottle.

Slipping in and out of consciousness, Jens lost the context of their conversation.

The old man spluttered. "So are you going to tell me your story?"

Heider paused. "All right, but this stays between us."

"Of course."

Heider continued, "What do I remember about Nigel?" Heider sighed. "Well, before we came out here we had a big house party. We all live together, see? Anyway, we had music, all our friends round, our girlfriends were there, and everyone was having a great time."

"Ok." the old man said.

Jens listened closely.

"I went up to my room, yeah? And when I got there what do I find?" Heider paused.

Jens imagined him looking at Nigel's body at this point in his story. What was coming next?

"That bastard right there, on top of my girlfriend."

"What did you do?"

"Nothing." Heider chuckled. "Didn't see me. Neither of them did."

A long pause. Water chugged through the pipes, someone wheeled a cart past the door and then there was a sustained *hoot* of a horn outside.

"So, did you do it?" the man said, breaking the silence.

Jens held his breath, frightened Heider might hear him listening in.

"Yeah," Heider said, almost whispering.

Jens's eyes widened, but he remained still. He wanted to scream. He'd never thought Heider would do such a thing. They were friends—best friends—and had been for almost all their lives.

"And what now?" the man said. "Are you going to tell your mate?"

Another pause. Heider whispered something.

"You have to be careful." the old man said. "You have to do it right."

"And you'll help me?"

"Yes," the old man said. "Have to admit I found myself in a pretty similar situation . . . a while back now."

They clinked their glasses then the chairs creaked back from the table. Jens turned over in his sleeping bag to see Heider and the old man approaching on tiptoe—Heider clutching the old man's meat cleaver.

MARSH

Now

TERRY CULLUM lies on his side punching the car door. He rolls over a little and gives it a few kicks. Finally it gives and creaks open to let in the late-afternoon sun. He reaches over to Julie and rocks her shoulder. For a few moments it seems like she won't wake, but then her eyelids flicker and her dark brown eyes gleam back at him. She has a cut on her forehead but the blood flow is under control and it just sticks there like the filling of a jam doughnut.

Terry yanks himself over the seat and out of the car. He lands on his feet, letting his knees take the force out of the drop. Mud seeps up his jean legs and sends a chill through his bones. He reaches back into the car, which lies on its side in the ditch, and he helps Julie out.

Together they collapse onto the side of the ditch. Terry takes in the scene. The other car is wrapped around a lamppost and there's no sign of the other driver, so he presumes they are still behind the wheel, perhaps unconscious or worse. His heart tickles his throat and he feels giddy like this has all unfolded in a dream, and he has only to pinch himself and he'll wake up.

He pinches but he doesn't wake up.

Terry pads his jacket pocket and feels the box there. He dips his hand inside and withdraws it, holding it up to the light. The box itself is unaffected by the crash and so he hopes too the contents were kept safe. He looks down at the box in his hand and then makes up his mind.

He wipes his hands, which are a little muddy, on the sides of his jeans and then turns to Julie. Her eyes widen and her mouth latches open. He opens the box to reveal a ring. Its green stone sparkles in the daylight. Neither of them have to say anything. It's too obvious what the gesture means what Terry has put into actions for lack of words. Julie leans forward and takes him in her arms, sobbing silently into his neck.

TERRY GRIPS THE WHEEL tightly and grits his teeth. This whole trip has just been one long pissing piss-take and he's looking forward to getting home, putting up his feet on his leather sofa and unwinding with a can of lager and the football highlights. The whole day is spoiled and there's no way that he can ever get back what he felt this morning, when he made the decision.

Julie sits in the passenger seat, her arms crossed against her chest, pouting and looking out the window. Her cheeks are lightly flushed from shouting and a few tear tracks linger on her skin, shining like snail trails.

Terry turns off down a country lane, preferring the rolling scenery to the main road.

Julie turns away from the window, scowling. "Why the hell are you going this way?"

"Just feel like it."

"But it takes another ten minutes."

He glances at her out of the corner of his eye. "I'm sorry, I didn't realise you had plans."

She rolls her eyes and turns away again. Under her breath, she says, "Should've bloody left me at Mum's if you're in a mood."

If there's one thing which riles Terry it's being told that he's in a mood when he's in a mood. But he doesn't react like in films, bringing the car to the halt and giving Julie a slap, he simply speeds up, going faster along the country road. A psychiatrist might call it passive-aggressiveness, but to Terry it just feels the natural thing to do.

He speeds around the corners, spilling over onto the other side of the road. He feels the weight on the wheel, followed by a light weightlessness when he temporarily loses all control of the car.

Julie reaches across, grips his arm. "Slow the hell down! You're going to get us both killed."

Terry smirks and pushes down on the accelerator, notching the speedometer over seventy miles an hour, lethal on a small road like this, if anything were to come the other way. He just doesn't care anymore, and will take whatever's coming to him. He probably deserves it.

Julie releases him. She grips her seatbelt and her lips part, perhaps saying something but the roar of the engine sucks the words right off her tongue.

Terry feels the backend of the car go but he holds it and keeps the tyres on the road, enjoying the buzz which passes through his chest afterward. He flies down the straightening road, leaving the ground whenever the car passes over a hump or incline.

Julie leans into him. "Stop the car! Stop the car!"

Terry reaches out and flips on the radio, spinning the volume knob round to maximum. A hiss of static fills the whole car. Terry's laughing, his smile tugging back the corners of his mouth. Julie is sobbing, her wails in chorus with the static.

At the end of the stretch the road heaves off to the left. Still chuckling away to himself, Terry pulls on the wheel, bringing the car face to face with another coming in the opposite direction. He stamps on the brakes and pulls back onto his side of the road. The other car skids past their window, Terry and the driver—a middle-aged man—lock eyes for a moment and then spin off in their respective trajectories. Terry guides the car back onto the road and then the wheels skid and the car hops the curb and crashes into the long grass.

Into the marsh.

TERRY DROPS THE HAMMER. It falls on his toe and sends flickers of pain all the way up his spine. Excruciating. He swears at the top of his voice. From within the house he hears the sound of footfall followed by a shout, his girlfriend, Julie. "Don't you dare swear here, Terry!"

Terry swears again under his breath. He snatches up the hammer and runs a quick fantasy through his head. Moments later he's through with it and back to doing his best to fix the rack for the hosepipe on the garage wall.

Julie's footsteps grow louder and she stands in the entrance to the garage. She speaks in a low voice this time. "Can't you behave? Mum can hear everything you say down here. Up there"—she gesticulates to the roof, to her mother's bedroom which sits above the garage—"it's like a pissing echoplex."

Terry grins. "And look who's swearing now."

"I'm not bellowing it at the top of my lungs."

Terry hammers the nail into the wall and then, faintly satisfied that he's finally got the job done, he steps back, picks up the hosepipe and hangs it on the nail. It remains there for approximately five seconds before gravity has its way, bending the nail and causing the hosepipe to crash onto the ground in a heap, like downed snake. "Pissing hell," Terry says, and flings the hammer across the garage where it clatters into the garage door, leaving a sizable dent.

Julie doesn't say anything this time, she just sighs and makes off back into the house.

Terry stares at the hosepipe lying on the ground, rubs his temple and swears again, this time loud enough that he's sure that not only the old bitch but the neighbours, and the neighbours' neighbours, can hear.

He's had enough and he storms out of the garage, through the house to his car which sits in the drive. He fishes out his car keys and opens it up. He sits in the driver's seat, staring out over the wheel knowing that he can go anywhere he wants now. Just a case of turning the key and flattening the accelerator.

Julie's voice pierces the air. Terry examines his wing mirror. She trots down the garden path wearing her yellow summer dress, the one which he likes—which he *really* likes—and before he can start the car she's thrown herself in front of it and stands there looking at him sternly.

For a few seconds Terry contemplates switching on, driving away. He's sure that she would get out of his path if she was sure he was going to drive. But he knows that he won't leave. Not without her.

Julie rounds the car, opens the passenger door and sits herself down in the seat. She closes the door behind her and stares holes in Terry's head. He chews on his tongue and then turns the ignition.

"What are you doing?" Julie says, her eyes wide and lips peeled back.

"I'm getting out of here."

Julie slaps the dashboard. "No! We haven't said goodbye! Mum's expecting us to stay for dinner at least."

"I'm not saying goodbye to that old bitch, let alone pissing away my time waiting for her crappy casserole or whatever she's baking in her witch's kitchen. He pulls out of the drive and heads for the road, looks both ways and then speeds up into the main road. He checks his mirror and then glances to Julie. This time he has a tear in his eye, turning everything a touch sparkly. "She can rot away for all I care."

Julie sinks back in the seat, shaking her head.

Terry examines the sign and makes for the smaller country roads. When he's wound up he likes to drive up into the hills, get his mind straight. If he's lucky Julie won't notice his detour until it's too late, less time efficient, to turn around and take the motorway. In a way he wishes Julie weren't even with him right now, that she hadn't come out to him—just stayed with her bag of crap mother.

Two Hours Before The Crash

TERRY LISTENS for Julie's footsteps to head down the stairs. He's alone with her mother now, in her bedroom. Her mother's prancing about reordering the place, making him move the furniture and get things in the order she likes. Ordinarily Terry doesn't put up with this but today he has a question emblazoned on his lips and he'll be damned if he's not going to get an answer to it. In fact he's spent the whole week wondering about this situation, trying to get her alone, and now seems as good a time as any with Julie out of earshot.

She looks over him, her lips pursed and gaze full. "There's something on your mind, isn't there?"

He thinks about how mother-in-laws have some kind of Jedi mind trick inbuilt into them, at least it means that he won't have to suffer too much if she can divine the answers from him.

She lets out a long sigh. "She's pregnant, isn't she?"

"Uh, what? No, of course not!"

She takes a step closer, her eyes sending prickles shimmering over his skin. God he wants to get out of this room, away from this oppressive woman and her bullying demeanour. Her breath is hot on his throat and her eyes twitch about their sockets. "Then what?"

Terry gulps in the air, touches his pocket and then straightens up, looking her right in the eye so that he's convinced she won't be able to deny him, not once he's got the question out. Now he's resolved not only that he should get the question out but that she will reply in the affirmative. He opens his mouth. "I was wondering—"

"You want to marry her, don't you?"

He doesn't break off eye contact, resolved that if it's the last thing he'll ever do in his life he will keep on looking into those lifeless black eyes, until he hears the answer which he requires.

"Go on, admit it then. Say it out loud."

"I want to marry Julie."

She lets out a long, sustained exhale. Her eyes shoot to her shoes and then to the wall, finally they rest on him, looking right into his and burning holes in the back of my skull. "I don't think it would be appropriate."

For a few moments Terry's speechless, not knowing how in the hell to respond to that question. He steels himself and gets himself under control to utter, "What do you mean that it wouldn't be appropriate?"

"Look, I've gone along with this . . . this thing for a long time now, and I've stayed quiet about my feelings surrounding you and Julie, not told her that she's wasting her time."

Terry's throat dries up. He can't believe that Julie's mother actually has the nerve to say these words out loud and, at the back of his mind, he's forming an irrepressible and unstoppable rage which threatens to ball right out of him.

"What is it you do again?"

"I'm a cobbler."

"Right," she says, and then almost spits, "A cobbler."

He eyes her again. "I really love her and want to marry her." Another knot forms in his throat. "I've bought the ring."

"Well, that was somewhat premature." She waves her hand, as if swatting a fly. "If you came here wanting my blessing to ask for Julie's hand in marriage then you're going to be disappointed. But I don't begrudge Julie her choice, if she really does want to marry you then so be it."

He stands his ground another few seconds and then gets himself into shape realising he can't stand there the rest of his life, in front of Julie's mother, looking like a lemon. So he shifts out the room and heads downstairs.

He passes Julie halfway down and he turns on his side, not daring to look her in the eye lest she somehow divine what conversation he just had with her mother. But, in the end, it's impossible and he meets her eyes, beautiful, pale blue crystals.

"What's the matter, Terry?"

"No . . . nothing," he says, shifting past her, getting down to the foot of the staircase.

She hovers there, halfway up the stairs, and then shakes her head and climbs her way up to the top.

Terry props himself against the banister considering his options. Everything seems to be telling him to run the hell away, get out of the house and back to the safety of his own. Can he really keep up the charade with Julie if her mother's so opposed? Maybe she's noticed something which he's neglected to see about himself, perhaps it's like he suspected all these years and he's inadequate.

He heads back into the garage, surrounds himself with tools and gets to work on a hook for the hosepipe which lies coiled on the cold ground like a resting snake.

Author's Note

Thank you for taking the time to read one of my books. If you would like to hear about my latest releases you can sign up for my newsletter here: www.aviain.com

Thanks for reading!

AV Iain

Crime & Creeps
A Short Story Collection